"My favorite part is when Hilo travels through galaxies. If I had to describe it in three words, I'd say it's **'SUCH A BLAST!'** D.J. is my favorite because he's a really good friend!"

—Matt A., age 10,
Bloomfield, N.J.

much! I really, **REALLY LOVE** the Hilo books."

—Angel O., age 10,
Brooklyn

"**GINA WAS MY FAVORITE** character because she's into science and soccer like me! I also liked D.J.'s family because it looks like mine!"

—Kiran M., age 7,
Carlsbad, Calif.

"*Hilo* is really cool and funny. It's **FUNNY** that he likes mangoes. You should read it because it's actually just **REALLY FUNNY!**"

—Gerard A., age 8,
Bloomfield, N.J.

"**HIGH ENERGY** and **HILARIOUS**!"

—Gene Luen Yang,
winner of the Printz Award

"FANTASTIC. EVERY SINGLE THING ABOUT THIS . . . IS TERRIFIC."

—Boingboing.net

"My students are obsessed with this series. **OBSESSED!**"

—Colby Sharp, teacher, blogger, and co-founder of the Nerdy Book Club

"More **GIANT ROBOTIC ANTS** . . . than in the complete works of Jane Austen."

—Neil Gaiman, author of *Coraline*

"Anyone who loves to laugh should read *Hilo*. It is **ACTION-PACKED** with a robotic touch."

—Breslin S., age 10,
Jackson, Mich.

"*Hilo* is loads of **SLAPSTICK FUN**!"

—Dan Santat,
winner of the Caldecott Medal

READ ALL THE HILO BOOKS!

HILO #1 THE BOY WHO CRASHED TO EARTH

HILO #2 SAVING THE WHOLE WIDE WORLD

HILO #3 THE GREAT BIG BOOM

HILO #4 WAKING THE MONSTERS

HILO #5 THEN EVERYTHING WENT WRONG

HILO #6 ALL THE PIECES FIT

HILO #7 GINA — THE GIRL WHO BROKE THE WORLD

HILO #8 GINA AND THE BIG SECRET

HILO #9 GINA AND THE LAST CITY ON EARTH

BOOK 9

HILO
GINA AND THE LAST CITY ON EARTH

BY JUDD WINICK

COLOR BY MAARTA LAIHO

RANDOM HOUSE NEW YORK

With thanks to Shasta Clinch, for her thoughtful feedback, insights, and perspective

Visit us on the Web! rhcbooks.com

Educators and librarians, for a variety of teaching tools, visit us at RHTeachersLibrarians.com

Library of Congress Cataloging-in-Publication Data
Names: Winick, Judd, author.
Title: Hilo. Book 9, Gina and the last city on earth / Judd Winick.
Description: First edition. | New York: Random House Children's Books, 2023. | Series: Hilo; book 9 | Audience: Ages 8–12. | Summary: "Gina saves the world and restores the earth to what it was before magic took over"—Provided by publisher.
Identifiers: LCCN 2021050275 (print) | LCCN 2021050276 (ebook) | ISBN 978-0-593-48809-6 (hardcover) | ISBN 978-0-593-48811-9 (library binding) | ISBN 978-0-593-48810-2 (ebook)
Subjects: CYAC: Graphic novels. | Magic—Fiction. | Imaginary creatures—Fiction. | Science fiction. | LCGFT: Graphic novels. | Science fiction.
Classification: LCC PZ7.7.W57 Hq 2023 (print) | LCC PZ7.7.W57 (ebook) | DDC 741.5/973—dc23/eng/20220202

The artist used digital medium to create the illustrations for this book.
The text of this book is set in 11-point ImaginaryFriend BB.
Book design by Bob Bianchini and Juliet Goodman

MANUFACTURED IN CHINA

10 9 8 7 6 5 4 3 2 1

First Edition

Dedicated to . . .

for believing in me.

TWO DAYS AGO.

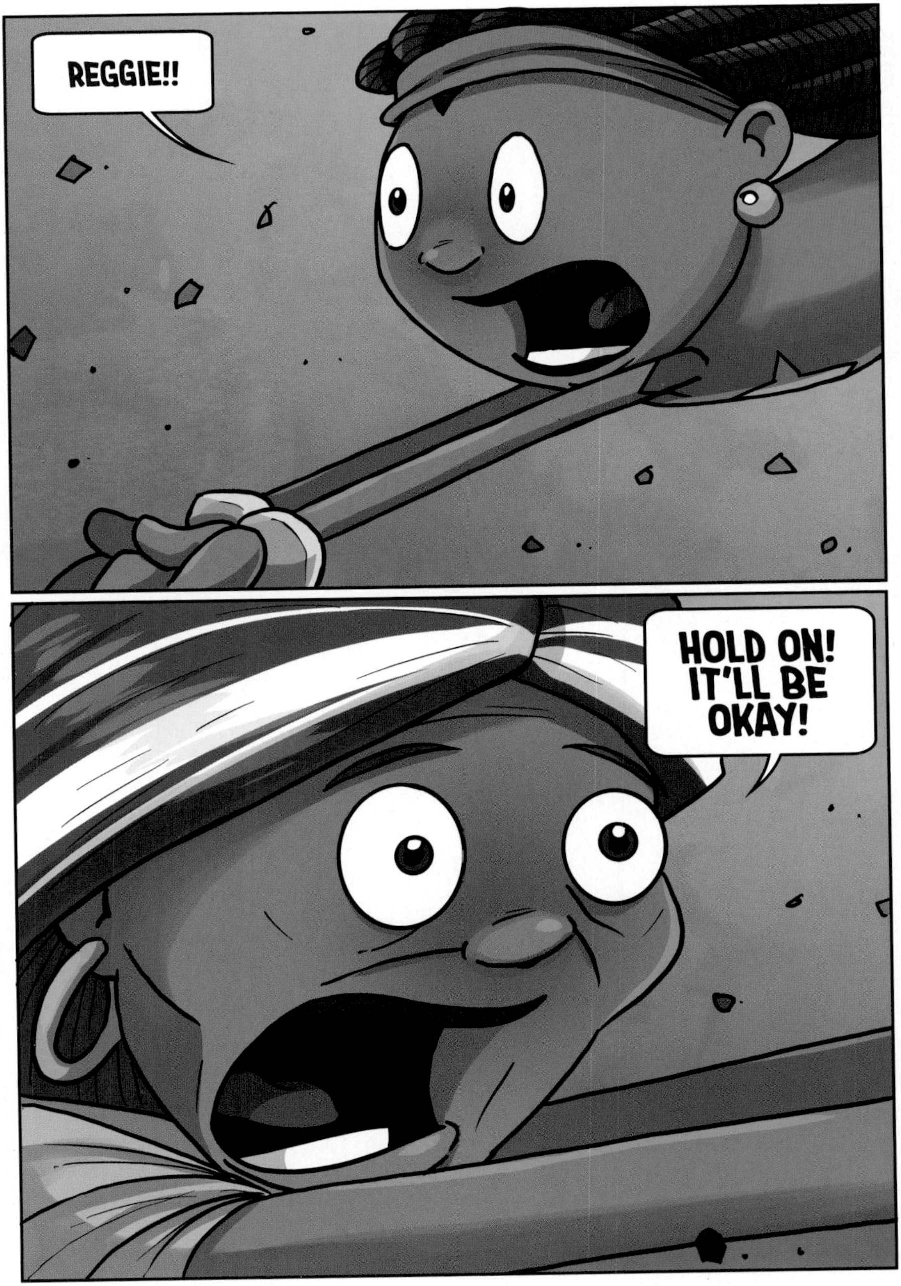

THIS DOESN'T **LOOK** OKAY.

IT WILL BE.
I PROMISE.

CHAPTER 1

REGINA LEE COOPER

AND MY LIFE IS
MAGICAL.

I FOUND MAGIC BECAUSE OF MY FRIENDS.
THERE'S D.J., MY OLDEST FRIEND.
POLLY, WHO COMES FROM ANOTHER PLANET. (THAT'S WHERE I LEARNED TO DO MAGIC FOR THE FIRST TIME.)
HAZZAH!!
STEP UP, KNUCKLEBUTTS.
AND POLLY'S BROTHER, PIP.
AND HILO AND IZZY. THEY WERE ROBOTS FROM ANOTHER WORLD. AND THEY ARE AMAZING.
WHAT'S THAT?
AN ELEPHANT THAT SNEEZES STRING CHEESE.
HWOONK
BUT NOT TOO LONG AGO, HILO BECAME HUMAN.
DO FEET ALWAYS SMELL THIS BAD?
THEY DO IF YOU DON'T WASH THEM.
GOOD MAN.
THEN I SHALL WASH THEM!

BUT WE LOST IZZY.

TO BE HONEST, WITH HER GONE, **NOTHING** HAS FELT THE SAME.
WE MISS HER **SO** MUCH.

AFTER IZZY, THINGS GOT... WELL... **COMPLICATED.**
THESE MAGICAL CREATURES CALLED **THE NESTOR** WENT BACK IN TIME THROUGH A PORTAL AND CHANGED THE HISTORY OF THE WORLD.
NOW IN THIS **NEW** HISTORY, THE EARTH HAS BEEN RULED BY **MAGIC** FOR **THOUSANDS** OF YEARS.
AND IT'S KIND OF MY FAULT.

REGGIE.
I DON'T KNOW **WHY** I FOUND MAGIC. BUT THE FIRST TIME IT HAPPENED, I WAS **SIX.**
WHUMP
ARE YOU OKAY?
YOU CAN **SEE** ME?
YES.

CAN ANYONE **ELSE** SEE ME?
HEY! CAN ANY OF YOU SEE THIS?
SEE WHAT?
NOPE.
AFTER **THAT,** I STARTED SEEING MAGICAL FOLKS NOW AND AGAIN.
MOST TIMES **OTHER** MAGICAL FOLKS WOULD SHOW UP AND TAKE THEM AWAY.

SOMETIMES QUIETLY.
YOU. OUT OF THE POOL. LET'S GO.
SOMETIMES NOT.
I NEVER UNDERSTOOD WHY I WAS THE ONLY ONE WHO COULD SEE THEM...
BUT I GOT THE FEELING THAT MAGICAL CREATURES WEREN'T SUPPOSED TO BE ON EARTH.
THEN I GOT IN THE HABIT OF HELPING OUT HERE AND THERE.
YEAH, YEAH. MOVE IT. YOU DON'T HAVE TO GO HOME, BUT YOU CAN'T STAY HERE.
AND I DID THAT FOR A LONG TIME.

YEARS LATER, LONG AFTER I WAS ALREADY A GRANDMOTHER, THERE WAS AN **EXPLOSION** AT A FACTORY. IT CAUSED A CAVE-IN UNDER THE BUILDING.
BOOM
I JUST GOT THE FEELING I **HAD** TO GO HELP.
I GOT THE TRAPPED WORKERS OUT...
BUT THE CAVE-IN OPENED A **MAGIC PORTAL.** I WALKED RIGHT THROUGH...
AND WOUND UP **HERE.**
THAT WAS WHEN I WAS ASKED TO BE **THE LOCK.**

AS THE LOCK, **MY** JOB IS TO STOP **ALL** MAGIC FROM COMING TO EARTH.
AAAAH!
TEEN

WOOOOOOOOOON
WHOA.
WHOA? WHY "WHOA"?
IT'S SOMETHING YOU SAY. I MEAN, "WHOA," LIKE "AMAZING"!
OH. IN MY DAY, "WHOA" WAS WHAT YOU SAID TO STOP A HORSE.
WHAT'S AMAZING IS ALL THAT YOU'VE BEEN THROUGH. MAGIC. GIANT MONSTER ROBOTS. SAVING THE WORLD.

AND YOU LOST YOUR FRIEND.
THAT IS **SO** MUCH WEIGHT TO CARRY.
AND **YOU** TOO, D.J. AND LISA. YOUR **FAMILY'S** BEEN MISSING SINCE THIS WORLD WENT SIDEWAYS.
I AM **SO** SORRY.
THANK YOU.
CAN YOU HELP GET THEM BACK?
ABSOLUTELY.
CRAKOOOOOOOM

I AM THE MIGHTY KRAVOOROON! DEVOURER OF WORLDS! THIS PUNY PLANET SHALL BE CRUSHED UNDER MY MIGHTY--
CHEEEEEEEEE
KRONK
FWOOSH

WHOA.
YEAH. STOP HORSE.
IS IT ALWAYS LIKE THIS?
NO. SOMETIMES IT'S REALLY BUSY.
THAT'S JUST MY JOB HERE IN THE CITY!
THE CITY?
HERE! THIS PLACE! SOME CALL IT THE MAYHEM. SOME CALL IT THE CROSSROADS. TO ME-- IT'S THE CITY.
WHUMP
AAAA AAAA AAH!
DO NOT MAKE ME CHASE YOU!

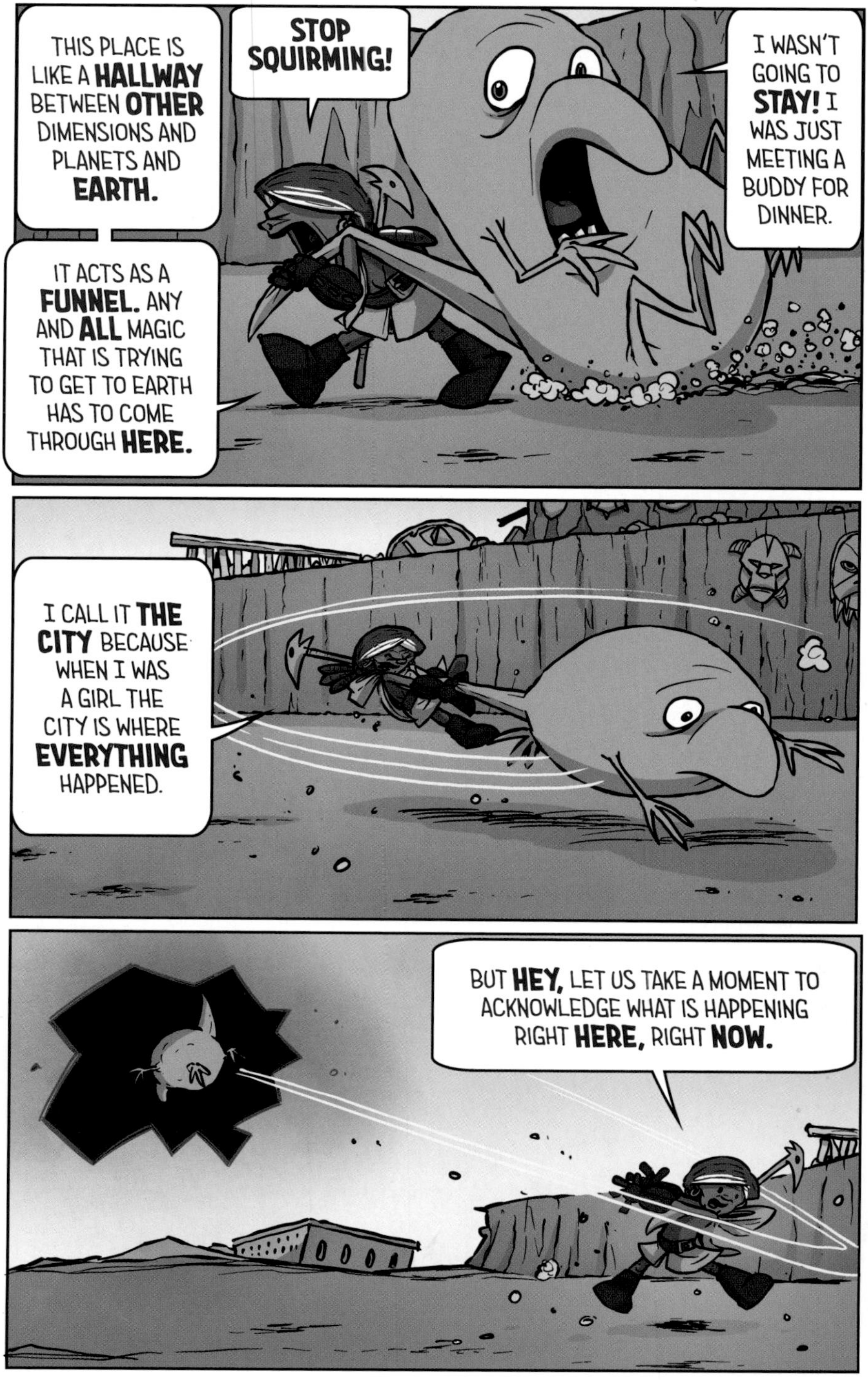
THIS PLACE IS LIKE A **HALLWAY** BETWEEN **OTHER** DIMENSIONS AND PLANETS AND **EARTH.**
STOP SQUIRMING!
I WASN'T GOING TO **STAY!** I WAS JUST MEETING A BUDDY FOR DINNER.
IT ACTS AS A **FUNNEL.** ANY AND **ALL** MAGIC THAT IS TRYING TO GET TO EARTH HAS TO COME THROUGH **HERE.**
I CALL IT **THE CITY** BECAUSE WHEN I WAS A GIRL THE CITY IS WHERE **EVERYTHING** HAPPENED.
BUT **HEY,** LET US TAKE A MOMENT TO ACKNOWLEDGE WHAT IS HAPPENING RIGHT **HERE,** RIGHT **NOW.**

YOU.
CHILD OF MY CHILDREN'S CHILDREN'S CHILDREN.
TIME, SPACE, MAGIC, THE UNIVERSE HAVE MANAGED TO COME TOGETHER PERFECTLY LIKE PIECES OF A CLOCK AND NUDGED THE GEARS TO SPIN.
FATE HAS BROUGHT YOU AND ME HERE TOGETHER IN THIS SAME PLACE.
MY LIFE HAS BEEN FILLED WITH SO MUCH THAT IS EXTRAORDINARY AND AWE-INSPIRING.
BUT I DON'T THINK ANYTHING CAN COMPARE TO THE SHOCK AND WONDER I'M FEELING RIGHT NOW.

HELLO, MY GREAT-GREAT-GREAT-GRANDDAUGHTER.
IT IS SO VERY VERY VERY GOOD TO SEE YOU.
YEEEEEE-HA!
HOLD ON FOR A SEC.

THESE ARE THE **FIRST** GUESTS I'VE HAD OVER IN A **LONG** TIME! **COULDN'T** YA WAIT?!
HOOM
BWEEEEEE

WHEEEEEE!
"WHEEEE"? SERIOUSLY?
HAHAHAHA. **BOOM BAH!**
OH, JUST **LOOK** AT HOW MAGIC RUNS IN OUR FAMILY.
HOW DID YOU LEARN TO DO A **TOPIARY SPELL** LIKE THAT?!
I NEVER LEARNED. IT JUST KIND OF HAPPENED.

NO ONE TAUGHT YOU?
WELL, WHEN I WAS ON OSHUN, THAT'S OUR FRIEND POLLY'S PLANET, IT WAS LOADED WITH MAGIC. SHE SHOWED ME A FEW THINGS.
AND THAT'S WHEN I STARTED.
MOSTLY I CAN DO STUFF WITH IVY AND BRANCHES AND LEAVES.
SHE ONCE MADE A WALL OF TREES THAT WAS LIKE THREE MILES LONG.
SHE CAN ALSO BLAST STUFF, AND SHE MADE A FEW FORCE FIELDS.
REALLY.

YEAH. AND SHE CAN FEEL MAGIC TOO.
OUR FRIEND HILO NOTICED THAT SHE COULD SENSE A LOT OF MAGIC GOING ON.
YOUR FRIEND HILO COULD FEEL THAT YOU COULD FEEL MAGIC?
YEAH.
IS THAT WEIRD?
NO, NOT WEIRD. I WOULD CALL IT EXTRAORDINARY.
AND MAGNIFICENT.

BUT MAYBE I'VE BEEN DOING MAGIC WRONG OR SOMETHING. IT WOULD EXPLAIN HOW I BROKE THE PLANET.
I DON'T KNOW WHAT Y'ALL EXACTLY MEAN BY BROKE.
AND I DON'T UNDERSTAND HOW THE WHOLE WORLD COULD'VE BEEN TAKEN OVER BY MAGIC, AND I DIDN'T KNOW ABOUT IT. THERE ARE SOME UNBREAKABLE LAWS OF MAGIC THAT--
YOU TWO ARE TRIMPILANS, THIRD-LEVEL NUISANCE DEMONS, RIGHT?
YEAH.
YOU ALL HAVE SIX ARMS.
YEAH?
YOU'RE SUPPOSED TO HAVE SEVEN.
AW NUTS.

RAAAAAAAAAARGH!
BROOM
RAAA ARGH!
AREN'T YOU GOING TO STOP ME?
NOPE. GO AHEAD. INVADE EARTH.

WELL. MAYBE I'LL JUST INVADE EARTH A LITTLE LATER.
TWEEN
POOF
TWEEN
TWEEN
POOF
DANG IT. HOW GOOD ARE YOU AT LIFTING GLAMOUR SPELLS?
OH, YOU MEAN WHEN MAGIC DISGUISES ITSELF? OR HIDES STUFF? I DON'T REALLY KNOW.
I FEEL LIKE YOU'RE REALLY GOOD AT GLAMOUR SPELLS.

TRY THIS **WITH** ME. LEAN IN. **CONCENTRATE.**
THINK ABOUT **FORCING** THE CITY TO SHOW ITS **TRUE SELF.**
TRUE SELF?
YES. THINK **HARD,** KIDDO.
TWOOOOOOOOOOOOOO

HWEEEEEEEEEEEEEE
AW, BUTTERNUT. I HAVE BEEN SEEEERIOUSLY SHNOOKERED.
SOMEONE MANAGED TO STEAL THE ENTIRE CITY. IT'S GONE.
THE GLAMOUR SPELL FAKED EVERYTHING! I THOUGHT I'D BEEN SENDING MAGIC BACK TO WHATEVER DIMENSION IT CAME TROTTING OUT OF--BUT IT'S ALL BEEN AN ILLUSION! I'VE BEEN BAMBOOZLED.

SOMEONE'S BEEN SENDING **PHONY** MAGICAL CREATURES FOR ME TO DEAL WITH.
BOOYAH!
HWOOM
WHUUMP
PHONY.
HWEEN
POOF
AND **TIME** MOVES **REALLY** FUNNY HERE IN THE CITY. I DON'T KNOW HOW LONG IT'S BEEN **FAKE!** THIS MIGHT'VE BEEN GOING ON FOR A DAY, A WEEK, OR A YEAR.
AND... THE WORLD'S BEEN TAKEN OVER BY MAGIC...
A **ROYAL FAMILY** OF EVIL NUT BARS ARE RULERS OF EARTH.
AND, GINA, THEY **CAPTURED** YOUR MOTHER AND FATHER AND SISTERS.

YOU WERE RIGHT! I WAS WRONG, BIRDIE!
BIRDIE?
SORRY. YOU REMIND ME OF MY GRANDDAUGHTER. YOUR GREAT-GRANDMOTHER. HER NAME WAS STARLING. I CALLED HER BIRDIE.
IT'S OKAY. I DON'T MIND.
OKAY.
NOW! TIME TO GO FIX THE WORLD!
LET'S MEET UP WITH YOUR FRIENDS. ESPECIALLY YOUR ROBOT BUDDY WHO ISN'T A ROBOT ANYMORE. I REALLY WANT TO MEET HIM.
HILO.

CHAPTER 2

HUSH

THIS PLACE IS **REALLY** BIG!
AND IT SMELLS **A LOT** BETTER THAN YOU'D EXPECT FOR A GIANT ANCIENT CASTLE!
THE QUEEN.
STOP HIM!
I'M **TRYING!** HE'S **REALLY** FAST AND NONE OF THE SPELLS ARE **WORKING** ON HIM!
PRINCE ZACHARIAN.
FUTURE MONARCH OF EARTH.

DIDN'T HURT!
DIDN'T HURT!
DIDN'T HURT!
THAT IS A **REALLY** NICE PAINTING!
IT'S A **PROPHECY!**
DON'T **TELL** HIM THAT!
DO YOU THINK **HE'S** THE OTHER **MAGICAL HUMAN** IN THE PROPHECY?!
IT'S SUPPOSED TO BE **TWO HUMANS** WHO CAN DO MAGIC! HE DOESN'T SEEM TO BE ABLE TO **DO** MAGIC! IT JUST SEEMS LIKE **WE** CAN'T DO MAGIC TO **HIM!**

CRASH
CLAP

DID YOU EVEN TRY TO JUST GRAB HIM?
PRINCESS ASHLINASCENT. FUTURE MONARCH OF EARTH.
YOU'RE PRETTY STRONG.
THANK YOU.
THOSE ARE REALLY NICE SHOES.
THANK YOU.
HE'S INCREDIBLY POLITE.
WHERE ARE YOUR FRIENDS? WHERE'S THE GIRL WHO CAN DO MAGIC?
RIGHT NOW? DON'T KNOW. BUT IF I DID, I WOULDN'T TELL YOU. Y'ALL KNOW THAT.
CAN YOU FORCE IT OUT OF HIM?
NO. HE'S IMMUNE TO MAGIC.

I CAN BEAT HIM UP. **MAKE** HIM TALK.
ZACH. **YOU** COULDN'T BEAT AN **EGG.**
HE'S A **KID!** YOU'RE NOT BEATING UP A **KID!**
SO? WHAT ARE WE GONNA DO WITH HIM?
AND UNTIL YOU TELL US **WHERE** YOUR **FRIENDS** ARE--
YOU WILL **ROT** HERE!

OKAY. BUT I'M NOT GONNA TELL YOU. SO IT MIGHT BE A **LONG** TIME. CAN I GET A BOOK TO READ?
WHAT DO YOU LIKE TO READ? DANNY'S GOT **A LOT** OF ROMANCE NOVELS.
THEY'RE **NOT** ROMANCE NOVELS! THEY ARE HISTORICAL FICTION!
THERE'S A LOT OF **KISSING** IN THEM.
HE'S NOT GETTING A BOOK!
I **AM** A LITTLE HUNGRY. DO YOU HAVE MANGOES? OR COOKIES?
WE GOT COOKIES. MACAROONS OKAY?
I WAS **SAVING** THOSE.
WE'RE **NOT** GIVING HIM **COOKIES!** Y'ALL ARE **REALLY** BAD AT PUTTING PEOPLE IN DUNGEONS!

I HONESTLY DIDN'T KNOW WE HAD A DUNGEON DOWN HERE. I THOUGHT THESE WERE BATHROOMS.
IS THERE ANY PLACE IN THIS CASTLE YOU DON'T USE AS A TOILET?
YOU REALLY WANT ME TO ANSWER THAT?
YOU NEED TO FIGURE OUT HOW WE CAN GET ANSWERS OUT OF HIM. I WANT THAT GIRL WHO CAN DO MAGIC. I WANT THIS ALL DONE BEFORE THE CORONATION.
I HEARD ABOUT THE CORONATION. YOUR FATHER WAS THE KING. AND HE DIED, RIGHT?
NOW YOU TWO ARE GOING TO BECOME THE KING AND QUEEN OF THE WORLD.
I'M VERY SORRY ABOUT YOUR DAD. THAT MUST HAVE BEEN HARD.
IT WAS.
THANK YOU.

MOM'S RIGHT. I DON'T WANT THIS LITTLE JERK AND HIS JERK FRIENDS RUINING THE CORONATION. WE'RE SO BEHIND IN THE PARTY PLANNING.
WE HAVE, LIKE, FIVE MORE DESSERTS TO DECIDE BETWEEN.
WILL YOU PLEASE STOP TALKING ABOUT THE DESSERTS?!
BUT THEY WANT TO SERVE FLAN. WHO LIKES FLAN?
I DO. I'LL TAKE FLAN INSTEAD OF THE COOKIES.
IF THE PROPHECY IS TRUE, THEN THERE'S TWO MAGICAL HUMANS OUT THERE WHO ARE GOING TO TAKE THIS WORLD FROM US.
WE ARE GOING TO FIND THEM BEFORE THEY CAN EVER, EVER DO THAT.
YOU WILL STAY HERE UNTIL YOU TELL US WHERE YOUR FRIENDS ARE!!

OKAY.

YOU COULD LEAVE HERE ANYTIME YOU WANT.
HUSH.

CHAPTER 3

BATTLE ROYALE

WE'LL GET HIM AND MY FAMILY BACK.
HOW COULD YOU **LET** THEM **TAKE HIM?!**
WE DIDN'T **LET** THEM! HE **JUMPED** ALL WILLY-NILLY INTO A **PORTAL** THAT THEY ESCAPED IN!
YOU **KNOW** THAT BOY'S ALL FLIBBERTIGIBBET! IT'S **IMPOSSIBLE** TO STOP HIM FROM DOING **ANYTHING.** EVEN IF HE IS **HUMAN** NOW.
AND HE TALKS ABOUT POOPING A LOT.
AND HE TALKS ABOUT POOPING **A LOT.**
NOT THE POINT! WE'RE GOING TO GET HIM **RIGHT NOW!**
WE WILL.
WASN'T THERE A BUNCH OF **GANGSTER MONSTERS** TRYING TO **KILL** US?
THEY'RE GAMBLING WITH PIP.

ALL BETS DOWN, LADDIES! ALL BETS DOWN!
YOUR LUCK'S **ABOUT** TO RUN OUT, YA HALF-PINT!
YOU KEEP THINKING THAT, **MELOK!** I'M GOING TO **OWN** YOUR METAL UNDERWEAR **RIGHT** AFTER THIS NEXT TURN!
WHERE'S THE ROYAL CASTLE?
ABOUT A THOUSAND MILES FROM HERE.
CAN YOU **TELEPORT?**
SURE.
YOU CAN **TALK?!**
THIS IS A **BEARACAT.** THEY CAN **ALL** TALK. AND MOST TELEPORT.
HOW COME YOU NEVER SPOKE BEFORE?
DIDN'T HAVE ANYTHING TO SAY.

I NEED YOU TO TELEPORT US ALL TO THE CASTLE.
HEY! THAT BEARACAT BELONGS TO MELOK THE DESTROYER! NOT YOU!
ACTUALLY, BENNY, PIP WON ALL THE BEARACATS IN THE LAST ROUND. AND YOUR BOOTS.
GIVE IT UP THERE, SUNNY JIM.
OKAY! LET'S GO! MOVE, MOVE, MOVE! TIME TO GO GET HILO!
IS HE ALWAYS THIS ENERGETIC?
WHEN HILO'S IN TROUBLE? YES.
SO WE'RE GOING TO THE CASTLE AND WE'RE GONNA FIGHT THEM TO GET HILO BACK?

OH! I'VE ALWAYS WANTED TO STORM A CASTLE!
TOO RIGHT! I HOPE THEY HAVE A DRAGON! A DRAGON FIGHT IS THE BEST KIND OF FIGHT YOU CAN FIGHT!
YOU'RE A WEIRD KID.
TO TAKE DOWN THE CASTLE WE'RE GOING TO NEED AN ARMY OF ZOMBIES AND AT LEAST ONE GIANT SNAIL THAT CAN BARF ACID.
AYE! THEN IT'S DRAGON TIME!
WE'RE NOT ATTACKING THE CASTLE.
RIGHT?
RIGHT. WE'RE JUST GOING TO TALK TO THIS ROYAL FAMILY.
OH? TALK TO THEM? BECAUSE THEY DID TRY TO DESTROY US.

YES. BUT WE DON'T KNOW WHY. THEY RULE THIS WORLD AND THEY PROBABLY HAVE ANSWERS.
THERE'S AN EXCELLENT CHANCE THAT THEY MIGHT BE AGREEABLE ONCE WE EXPLAIN WHAT HAPPENED.
ARE WE JUST TAKING THIS ONE BEARACAT?
WE JUST NEED THE ONE TO GET US THERE.
AND SALLY HERE DOESN'T REALLY GET ALONG WITH THE OTHER BEARACATS.
JANET'S RUDE.
I AM NOT!
LET'S GO!
GOING!
BWEEEE-EN

BOMF
WHOA!
STOP HORSE!
WHUMP

THAT WAS A PRETTY BUMPY LANDING.
WHAT HAPPENED? WHERE IS THE CASTLE?
I COULDN'T GET ALL THE WAY THERE. THERE'S A BARRIER BLOCKING ANYONE FROM TELEPORTING CLOSER.
MAYBE WE COULD WALK THE REST OF THE WAY.
I DON'T THINK SO.
I AM QUEEN VALETUDO OF THE ROYAL HOUSE OF MALUM. YOU ARE ATTEMPTING TO TRESPASS UPON SACRED GROUND!

WHERE'S OUR FRIEND HILO?!
BLOND HAIR. RED T-SHIRT. EXTREMELY POLITE.
OI. THAT'S SOME OF THE BAG OF NINNYHAMMERS THAT TRIED TO TAKE US APART.
YEAH. LET'S KICK THEIR BUTTS SO FAR THEY WON'T BE ABLE TO FIND THEM WITHOUT A FLASHLIGHT AND A MAP!
TAKE IT EASY. LET ME DO THE TALKING.
WE'RE JUST DOING A LITTLE FACT-FINDING. WE'RE TRYING TO FIND OUT HOW THE ROYAL FAMILY CAME TO POWER IN THIS WORLD.
AND NOBODY TELL THEM I'M THE LOCK. THEY ARE ALL ABOUT MAGIC, AND MY JOB IS TO STOP MAGIC. THAT WILL MAKE THEM... NERVOUS.
SO EVERYONE STAY CALM.

HELLO! GOOD DAY! I'M REGINA. THIS IS MY GRANDDAUGHTER GINA.
HEY.
I THINK YOU'VE MET HER AND HER FRIENDS. THERE MIGHT HAVE BEEN A SMALL MISUNDERSTANDING. A BIT OF A KERFUFFLE.
BUT MOST IMPORTANTLY, WE ARE LOOKING FOR THE CHILDREN'S LOST FRIEND AND GINA'S FAMILY. ARE THEY AT THE CASTLE?
AND YOUR CASTLE IS SO BEAUTIFUL! MAGNIFICENT! HOW LONG HAVE YOU ALL BEEN LIVING THERE?
SNEAKY.
THANK YOU.
THAT'S HER. THAT'S THE GIRL WHO CAN DO MAGIC.
IF THE GRANDMOTHER CAN DO MAGIC, THEN THESE ARE THE TWO HUMANS...
THEY ARE THE PROPHECY.

TURN THE GIRL OVER TO US, AND WE WON'T DESTROY ALL OF YOU.
BUT WE ARE GOING TO DESTROY THEM, RIGHT? I PUT MY ARMOR ON BECAUSE I THOUGHT WE WERE GONNA BE DESTROYING THINGS.
THIS IS A GRANDMOTHER AND A BUNCH OF KIDS. WE'RE GOING TO DESTROY THEM?
WE DON'T HAVE TIME FOR THIS! THIS HAS TO BE SETTLED BEFORE THE CORONATION!
WHY DOES THIS HAVE TO BE SETTLED BEFORE THE CORONATION?
NONE OF US WANT ANY TROUBLE. ALL WE WANT TO DO IS TALK. ALL WE WANT TO DO IS UNDERSTAND WHAT HAPPENED HERE.
WHAT DOES SHE MEAN WHAT HAPPENED HERE?

YOU DO NOT GET TO ASK QUESTIONS, HUMAN!
WATCH YOUR TONE, YA BOBSNOPPLE! THIS IS THE LOCK YOU'RE TALKING TO!
DIDN'T I SAY NOT TO SAY THAT?
THE LOCK?!
GRANNY IS MAGICAL TOO?
THE MAGICAL HUMAN FROM THE PROPHECY IS THE LOCK?!
DESTROY THEM!!
GAME ON, BABY!!

ROOOAAR

SPROONG

CROOOM
CROOOM

THEY ARE NOT SUPPOSED TO BE THIS POWERFUL! SOMETHING IS DEEPLY WRONG HERE!
COOM
COOM
GINA, WHO IS THE BEST FIGHTER BESIDES YOU?!
WHAT? I'M NOT THE BEST--
GINA! WHO IS THE BEST FIGHTER BESIDES YOU?!
POLLY.
POLLY.
ME!
POLLY.
WELL, YES, IT WOULD BE ME.

BWEEEEEEEN

SIC 'EM, KITTY!
OH! TOO RIGHT!

YOU WANT SOME LUNCH?!
HOW ABOUT A DIRT SANDWICH?!
THIS IS A LOT OF MAGIC COMING FROM TWO HUMANS AND SOME CATS!
SHUT UP AND FIGHT, ZACH!

HWIIIIIR
PIP! **COVER US!**
AHOY!
TZOT
TZOT
TZOT
TZOT
TZOT
OH, YOU'LL BE FEELING **THAT** TOMORROW, FROGGY!
CRUONK
CATCH YOUR BREATH, GRANDMA! I'LL GO HELP PIP!
NO! STAY RIGHT HERE! AND YOU NEED TO FOCUS!

FOCUS? WHAT DO YOU ME--?
GINA. YOU ARE MORE CONNECTED TO MAGIC IN A WAY I'VE NEVER SEEN BEFORE.
YOU'VE NEVER BEEN TAUGHT ANYTHING. BUT YOU CAN DO SO MUCH.
NO TAIL PULLING, YOU CHEAT!!
BOOM

YOU CAN **FEEL** THE MAGIC. AND **THAT'S** WHAT I NEED YOU TO DO **RIGHT NOW.**
I WANT YOU TO **LOOK** AT THE ROYAL FAMILY-- AND TELL ME WHAT YOU **FEEL.**
WHAT I **FEEL?**

YES! FOCUS! LOCK ONTO THEM! LOOK AT THESE MAGICAL BEINGS, DIG IN--
AND TELL US WHAT THEY ARE.
ZWEEEEEEEEEEEN
YOU! FIGHT! AS! BAD! AS! YOU! SMELL!
WHOCK WHOCK WHOCK WHOCK

WHAT DO YOU FEEL?
THEY'RE SCARED.
YES?
SOME OF THEM ARE MORE SCARED THAN OTHERS.
YES?
SOME OF THEM ARE LYING.
LYING ABOUT WHAT?
LYING ABOUT WHO THEY REALLY ARE.

CRASH
OKAY. TIME TO GET
CREATIVE!

UH-OH.
PLEEK
AW, BUTTERNUT. I'M A TREE.
HWONK

OI! I'M NOT GIANT ANYMORE AND GETTING BLASTED AT! YOU COULD'VE WARNED A CAT!
OH, C'MON.
THIS!
IS!
NOT!
GOOD!
HANG ON, GRANDMA!
SHOULD WE FOLLOW THEM?
NOT ME.
WHERE ARE YOU GOING?!
TO THE CASTLE! I'M GETTING HILO!

WAIT! HANG ON!
I'M COMING TOO!
PIP! YA MAD SQUEAKER! COME BACK!
WHUMP

YOU'RE A TREE.
YEAH. I'M WORKING ON THAT.
WHERE ARE D.J., LISA, AND PIP?
THEY TOOK OFF FOR THE CASTLE TO FETCH HILO.
WHAT?! WE HAVE TO GO AFTER THEM! WE--
DESTROY THEM!

BOMF

AAAAAARGH!
ARE WE DONE HERE? WE REALLY NEED TO CALL THE FLORIST.

CHAPTER 4

IT DOESN'T MAKE IT ANY LESS TRUE

I **DON'T** WANNA TALK ABOUT THIS AGAIN.
BUT WE **HAVE** TO.
NO, WE DON'T.
YOU DON'T HAVE TO STAY HERE.
YES, I DO.
NO. YOU CAN LEAVE **ANYTIME** YOU WANT.
IF I DO WHAT YOU'RE TELLING ME TO DO... I'LL **LOSE** YOU.
YOU'VE **ALREADY** LOST ME.
I DON'T WANNA LOSE YOU **AGAIN.**
BUT I'M **NOT** REALLY HERE.
YOU **ARE.** I'M **TALKING** TO YOU. I **SEE** YOU. I KNOW YOU'RE **THINKING.** I KNOW YOU'RE **FEELING.** I KNOW YOU'RE RIGHT **HERE** WITH ME.
BUT I'M **REALLY** NOT.

SNIFF
HOW CAN YOU NOT WANNA LEAVE HERE? THIS ROOM SMELLS TERRIBLE.
IF YOU'RE NOT HERE, HOW CAN YOU SMELL THE ROOM?
I CAN SMELL THE ROOM BECAUSE YOU CAN SMELL THE ROOM.
IT'S TIME FOR YOU TO BE WHO YOU'RE REALLY SUPPOSED TO BE.

I **DON'T** WANT TO LOSE YOU.
YOU'VE **ALREADY** LOST ME.
STOP SAYING THAT.
I CAN STOP SAYING IT.
BUT IT DOESN'T MAKE IT **ANY** LESS **TRUE.**

HEY.
WHO ARE YOU TALKING TO?
NO ONE.
I **JUST** HEARD YOU TALKING TO SOMEONE.
HE'S TALKING TO ME!
SHE CAN'T HEAR YOU.
YEAH, BUT SHE CAN HEAR **YOU.**
THERE. YOU JUST TALKED TO THEM **AGAIN!** I **HEAR** YOU HAVING A CONVERSATION.

SEE? SHE CAUGHT YOU.
HUSH.
ARE YOU HUSHING **ME** OR ARE YOU HUSHING THE SOMEONE THAT YOU'RE PRETENDING **NOT** TO BE TALKING TO?
ARE YOU IN THERE WITH A **GHOST?** WE **DO** HAVE GHOSTS IN THE CASTLE.
BUT THEY **USUALLY** JUST MOVE FURNITURE AROUND OR **SCREAM** AND TRY TO FREAK OUT THE CLEANING STAFF.
THAT SOUNDS KIND OF **MEAN.** PLEASE TELL HER I'M **NOT** A GHOST AND I WOULD **NEVER** DO THAT.
I WAS JUST A LITTLE BIT **LONELY,** AND I **TALK** TO MYSELF SOMETIMES. HAVEN'T YOU EVER DONE THAT?

MY MOM AND MY BROTHER ARE GOING TO FIND YOUR FRIENDS AND **DESTROY** THEM.
IF YOU TELL US WHERE THEY ARE, MAYBE WE CAN CAPTURE THEM WITHOUT **HURTING** THEM.
BUT YOU DID FIND THEM. AND THEY GOT AWAY. I **KNOW** THAT. I CAN **FEEL** THAT.
YOU CAN FEEL THAT BECAUSE **I** CAN FEEL THAT.
HUSH.

I DON'T KNOW WHO YOU'RE TALKING TO OR WHAT YOU'RE UP TO EXACTLY, BUT YOUR FRIENDS ARE IN DANGER...
YOU'RE NOT HELPING THEM BY DOING NOTHING.
SHE DOESN'T WANT TO HURT THEM.
WHAT?
SHE DOESN'T LIKE ANY OF THIS. I CAN FEEL IT.

WHAT? WHAT IS YOUR GHOST TELLING YOU?
THAT YOU THINK THIS IS WRONG.
SHE'S A BIT LIKE YOU.
IT'S TIME FOR HER TO BE WHO SHE'S REALLY SUPPOSED TO BE TOO.
WHAT?

CHAPTER 5

STEADY, BIRDIE

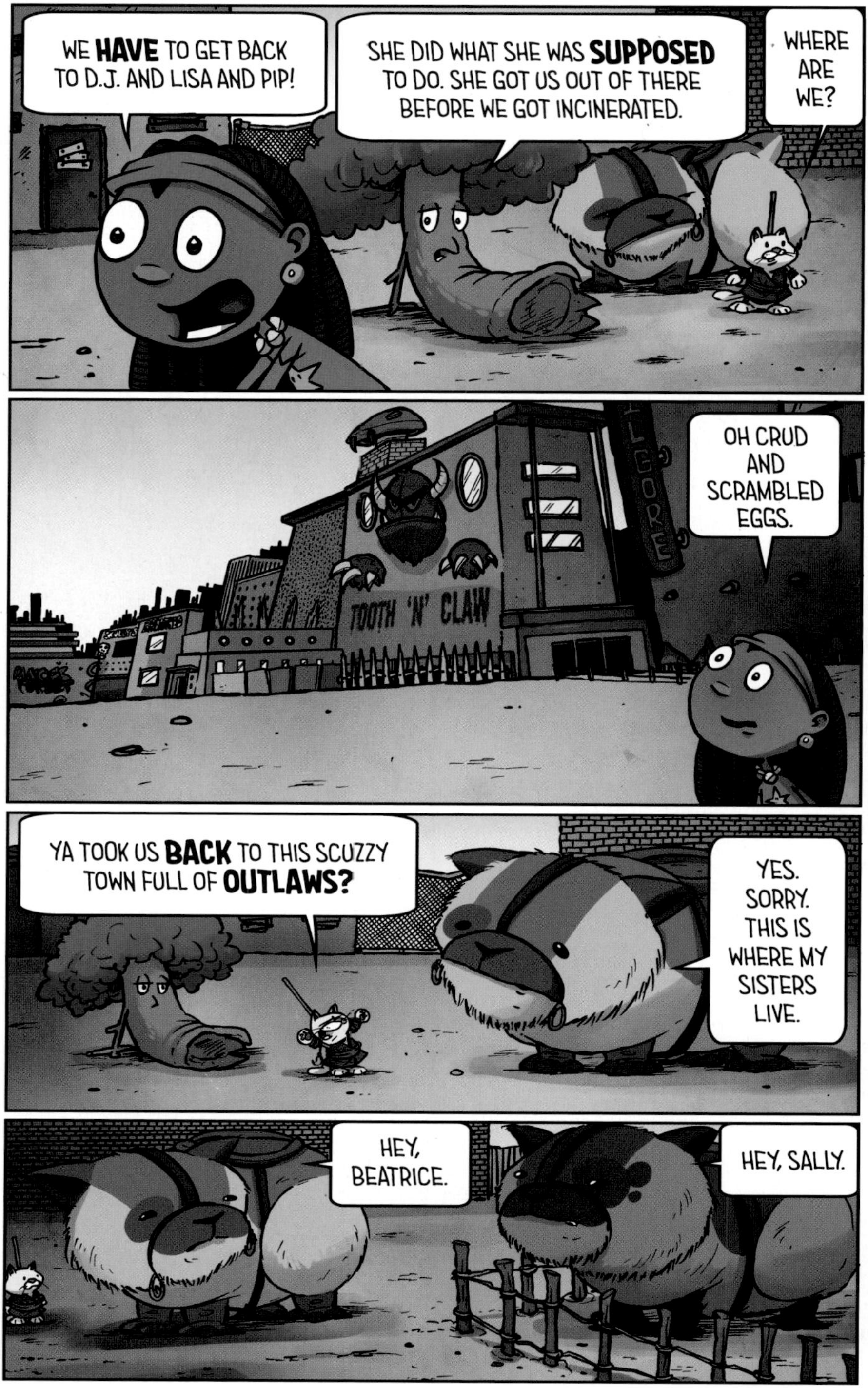
WE HAVE TO GET BACK TO D.J. AND LISA AND PIP!
SHE DID WHAT SHE WAS SUPPOSED TO DO. SHE GOT US OUT OF THERE BEFORE WE GOT INCINERATED.
WHERE ARE WE?
TOOTH 'N' CLAW
OH CRUD AND SCRAMBLED EGGS.
YA TOOK US BACK TO THIS SCUZZY TOWN FULL OF OUTLAWS?
YES. SORRY. THIS IS WHERE MY SISTERS LIVE.
HEY, BEATRICE.
HEY, SALLY.

ARE YOU OKAY?
NO. I'M A TREE.
POLLY, HOW ARE YOU AT **TRANSMOGRIFICATION** SPELLS? CAN YOU MAKE ME A HUMAN AGAIN?
I'M **TOP-NOTCH.** I'LL HAVE YOU BACK ON YOUR OWN TWO KICKERS IN A JIFFY.
HEY! **YOU'RE** THE LITTLE SNOT BUCKETS WHO TRASHED MY PUB!
NO. THAT WASN'T US! YOU MUST BE MISTAKEN!
THIS **IS** THEM! THAT'S THE CAT, AND THAT **HUMAN** MUST'VE BEEN **DISGUISED.**

POLLY, HURRY UP.
YOU CAN'T RUSH THESE THINGS. IF I BOTCH IT, SHE MIGHT GO FROM A TREE INTO A HAM SANDWICH.
I DO NOT WANT TO BE A SANDWICH.
I'M STILL CLEANING MUCUS OFF MY CEILINGS. DO YOU HAVE ANY IDEA HOW HARD IT IS TO CLEAN MUCUS OFF CEILINGS?
IT'S VERY HARD.
YEAH! VERY HARD!
LOOK, WE DON'T WANT ANY TROUBLE.
WHAT YOU WANT DON'T MATTER!
YEAH! TROUBLE IS WHAT YOU'RE GOING TO GET!
POLLY.
I NEED MORE TIME.

STEADY, BIRDIE.
I'VE GOT THIS.
ALL OF YOU...
PLEASE. JUST GIVE US SOME ROOM.
PLEASE.

CRAKOOM

HAZZAH.
HAZZAH IS RIGHT.

THERE. RIGHT AS RAIN.
OH, POLLY, THANK YOU.
HEY, FOLKS.

HUMAN BEING OVER HERE.
FOLLOW ME. WE'VE GOT A SAFE SPOT FOR YOU.
DO YOU THINK WE CAN TRUST HER?
I DON'T THINK WE HAVE MUCH CHOICE. WE HAVE TO GET OUT OF HERE.
BESIDES, IF ANYONE GIVES US ANY TROUBLE...
GINA CAN JUST EXPLODE WITH MAGIC AGAIN.
TOO RIGHT.

CHAPTER 6

WHEN PIGS FLY

WE COULD JUMP.
PIP.
I CAN MAKE IT. LET ME GET A RUNNING START.
NO! LOOK!
SEE THOSE FLYING CREATURES?
AYE! I'LL SNAG ONE OF THEM AROUND THE NECK AND DRAG THEM ON OVER. WE CAN FORCE THEM TO FLY US--
FWEET

HEY.
HEY.
COULD YOU FLY US TO THE CASTLE?
SURE.
SEE? ALL YOU HAVE TO DO IS ASK.
THAT'S WHAT MOM ALWAYS SAYS.
YEAH.

WE'RE **GOING** TO GET THEM BACK. MOM, DAD, JENNIFER, LOUIS, AND DEXTER.
ATTACK!
NO. WE'RE NOT GOING TO ATTACK **ANYONE.** WE'RE GOING TO THE CASTLE TO GET HILO BACK.
WE'RE GONNA GET THEM **ALL** BACK.
OI, PIG. DO YOU KNOW IF THEY HAVE ANY **DRAGONS** WE CAN FIGHT?
YOU **MUST** CHILL.

CHAPTER 7

TO BE A PART OF IT

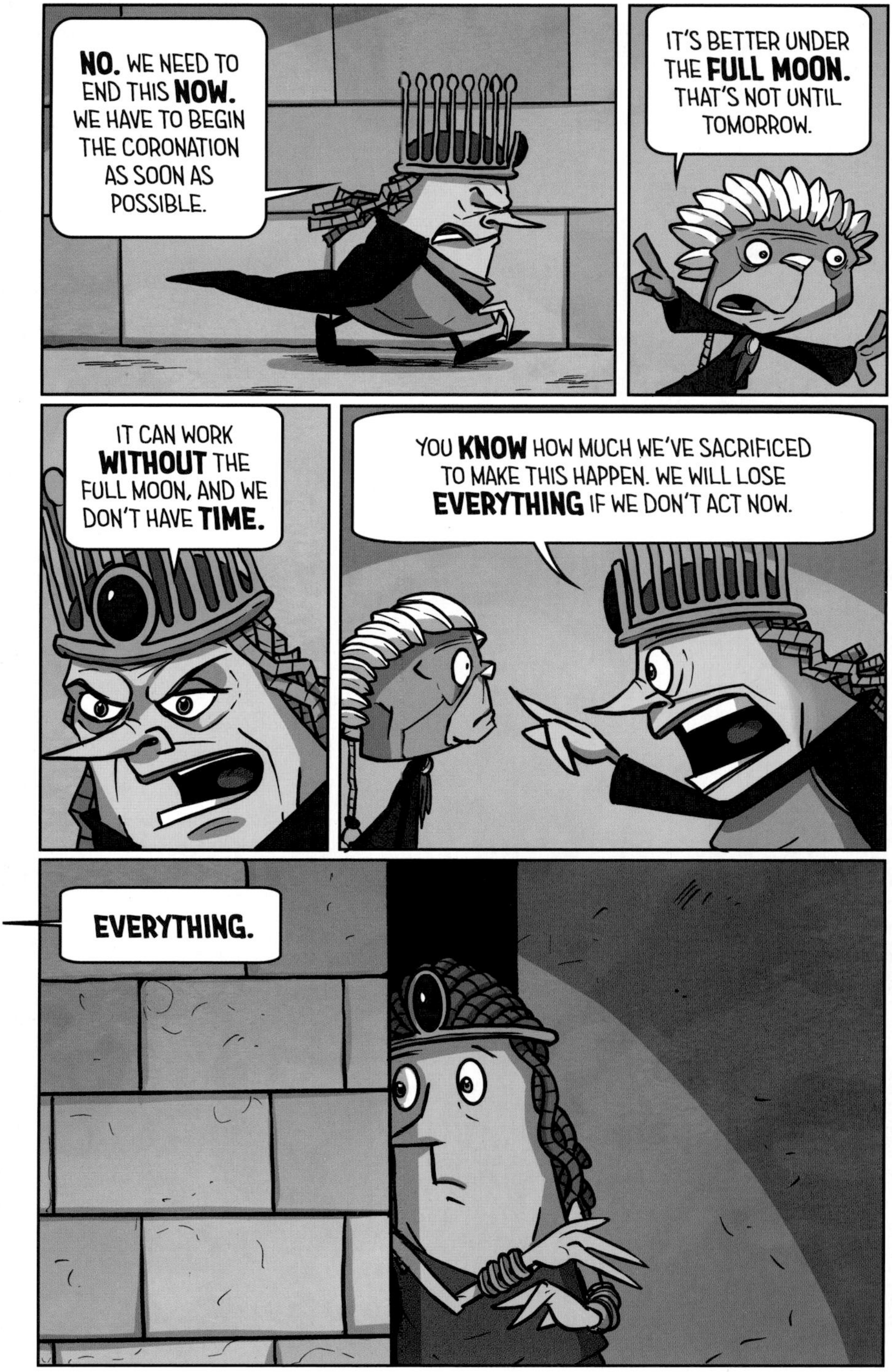
NO. WE NEED TO END THIS NOW. WE HAVE TO BEGIN THE CORONATION AS SOON AS POSSIBLE.
IT'S BETTER UNDER THE FULL MOON. THAT'S NOT UNTIL TOMORROW.
IT CAN WORK WITHOUT THE FULL MOON, AND WE DON'T HAVE TIME.
YOU KNOW HOW MUCH WE'VE SACRIFICED TO MAKE THIS HAPPEN. WE WILL LOSE EVERYTHING IF WE DON'T ACT NOW.
EVERYTHING.

CAN YOU DO **ONE** MORE?

OKAY. **ONE** MORE.

HEEEN
CWOOOOWNK
BAAAAH
AGAIN!

THAT'S EASY PEASY. I WAS A **GIANT** TWENTY MINUTES AGO.
THEY'VE NEVER SEEN HUMANS DO MAGIC.
WE'VE NEVER SEEN HUMANS DO MAGIC!
WE DON'T **REALLY** HAVE TIME FOR THIS.
YES. I KNOW YOU'RE ANXIOUS TO GET MOVING. AND WE **WILL.**
D.J. AND LISA ARE WITH **PIP.** HE'S YOUNG AND BRASH, BUT HE KNOWS HIS MAGIC, RIGHT?
WELL. IT JUST ABOUT **MURDERS** ME TO ADMIT THIS. BUT...
HE'S **PROBABLY** GOING TO BE A **BETTER** SORCERER THAN **ME.**

REALLY?
AYE! **REALLY!** SO WE DON'T NEED A **BIG** DISCUSSION ABOUT HOW MY **WEE** FAT-MOUTHED KNOW-IT-ALL SQUIRT OF A LITTLE BROTHER IS **STUPENDOUS** AT **MAGIC! OKAY?!**
AND I'M VERY PROUD OF HIM.
WOW.
YES. IT MAKES ME SICK.
SO THEY'RE IN **GOOD** HANDS FOR THE TIME BEING.
AND THAT **DOES** GIVE ME TIME TO CATCH MY BREATH.
AYE. REGGIE HERE TRANSMOGRIFIED FROM A **TREE,** AND THAT CAN BE **WOOLLY.**

SHE STILL MIGHT BE NEEDING A **FEW** MORE TICKS TO FINISH **COOKING.**
COUGH
AGAIN!!
POLLY, PERHAPS YOU COULD FIND ME SOME **DOG PATCH ROOT.** I COULD DO A **CLEANSING SPELL--**
YEAH! THAT'LL WORK LIKE A **RECONSTITUTION CHARM!**

CAN **WE** HELP? WE KNOW WHERE THERE'S A DOG PATCH!
LEAD THE WAY! I CAN TELL YA **ALL** ABOUT WHEN I WAS A GIANT TWENTY MINUTES AGO.
YOU KNOW **A LOT** OF MAGIC.
I KNOW **A LOT** OF MAGIC. I'VE HAD YEARS OF **PRACTICE.**
DID SOMEONE **TEACH** YOU?
SURE! ESPECIALLY IN THE BEGINNING.

I TOLD YOU THAT THERE WAS AN **EXPLOSION** IN THE FACTORY. AND I FOUND THIS **PORTAL.**
"IT JUST **CALLED** TO ME. I KNEW I **HAD** TO GO THROUGH IT."
"AND THEN I SAW **THE CITY...**"
"AND IT WAS LIKE **NOTHING** I'D EVER EVEN **IMAGINED.**"

"IT WASN'T JUST HOW BEAUTIFUL IT WAS... BUT I COULD FEEL HOW ALIVE IT WAS. HOW RICH. HOW POWERFUL. HOW CARING."
"I COULD FEEL HOW THIS WHOLE LAND... IT WANTED TO PROTECT OUR WORLD."
"AND I SO WANTED TO HELP."
"TO BE A PART OF IT."
"THEN SOMEONE SHOWED UP AND TOLD ME I COULD HELP."

"HIS NAME WAS TAMIR."
TAMIR?!
YOU KNOW HIM?
YEAH, WE KNOW HIM!

ON MY WORLD OF **OSHUN** HE WAS THIS BRUTAL **WARRIOR** FROM A THOUSAND YEARS AGO.
THEN HE BECAME A **TEACHER** AND **GUARDIAN** OF **PEACE.** HE BROUGHT MY ENTIRE **WORLD** TOGETHER.
AND HE GAVE THE SCIENTIST WHO **CREATED** HILO AND IZZY AN **ENERGY SOURCE.** IT'S THE **POWER** THAT **GAVE** THEM THEIR **POWERS.**
IT'S THE POWER THAT HELPED HILO AND IZZY **COME TO LIFE.**
THE EMPATIS.

MY GOODNESS. MY, **MY** GOODNESS. I HAD GUESSED THAT **MANY** THINGS BROUGHT US TOGETHER. BUT IT'S BEGINNING TO FEEL LIKE IN **ALL** THESE WAYS...
"IT MIGHT JUST BE **HIM.**"
SO, TAMIR TAUGHT YOU MAGIC.
OH, WHAT I WOULDN'T **GIVE** TO LEARN FROM TAMIR.
HE TAUGHT ME AT **FIRST.** THEN AS THE YEARS WENT ON, I LEARNED BY **DOING.**
"**AND** I LEARNED FROM **OTHER** FRIENDLY MAGICAL FOLK WHO DIDN'T MIND SHARING."

"BEING THE LOCK IS A HUGE RESPONSIBILITY. IT TOOK ME A LOOOOONG TIME TO GET GOOD AT IT."
GRANDMA REGGIE, HOW LONG HAVE YOU BEEN THE LOCK? BECAUSE, WELL--
YOU SHOULD BE WRINKLED LIKE A TURTLE'S KEISTER.
POLLY.
WHAT? AS OLD AS SHE IS? SHE SHOULD LOOK LIKE A SQUISHED PRUNE ON HOT PAVEMENT.
BUT TAKE A GANDER! SKIN AS SMOOTH AS A LAKE AT DAWN.

THANK YOU, CHILDREN. BUT **THAT'S** BECAUSE OF THE CITY.
TIME IS ALL KINDS OF **WABBY-DABBLY** THERE. IT DOESN'T WORK LIKE IT DOES ON **EARTH.** TIME SHRINKS AND STRETCHES. YESTERDAY COULD BE A HUNDRED YEARS AGO OR IT COULD BE TOMORROW. SO YOU **DON'T** EXACTLY AGE.
BUT HOW LONG **HAVE** YOU BEEN THERE?
THAT'S THE THING. I'M NOT SURE. MY **BEST** GUESS...
MAYBE **SIX HUNDRED YEARS.**

CHAPTER 8

DUNGEONS, NO DRAGONS

TUNK
YOU KNOW, FOR AN ANCIENT CASTLE, THIS DOESN'T SMELL TOO BAD.
OOCH. YA SHOULD SMELL IT WITH MY CAT HONKER. THIS PLACE REEKS LIKE BOILED SOCKS.
SNIIIIIIIF
BUT I CAN SMELL HILO.
YOU CAN SMELL HIM?
AYE. CAT PROBOSCIS. THEY'RE ABOUT FIFTEEN TIMES BETTER THAN YOU APES.

HILO'S DOWN THIS WAY. BUT--
SNIIIIIF
THERE'S A BUNCH OF GUARDS COMING.
WHAT?!
RUN.
NAH.

BWEEN
OI, FELLERS. HOW GOES IT TODAY?

Y'KNOW.
THE QUEEN HAS GOT US REWORKING THE CORONATION. SHE MOVED IT UP TO THIS AFTERNOON.
NOW WE HAVE TO CLEAN OUT THE ENTIRE EAST COURTYARD, LIKE, RIGHT NOW.
WHAT ARE Y'ALL UP TO?
OH, WE'RE JUST OFF TO CLEAN THE BASEMENT.
YOU MEAN THE DUNGEON?
YES. WE MEAN THE DUNGEON.
I THOUGHT WINSTON CLEANS THE DUNGEONS.
HE DOES. HE'S, UM, SICK.

REALLY? I JUST SAW HIM.
WELL, HE'S SICK NOW.
WHO TOLD YOU TO CLEAN THE DUNGEONS?
UM, PATRICE.
PATRICE? CAROL ANNE IS IN CHARGE OF THE CLEANING CREW IN THE LOWER DECKS, ISN'T SHE?
YEAH. PATRICE IS IN BUSINESS AFFAIRS.
RIGHT.
TZOT
TZOT
TZOT

WHUMP
WHUMP
WHUMP
SORRY. THEY WERE GETTING **REALLY** CHATTY.
TOTALLY.
LET'S GO.
AND HEY, **WHY** IS **MY** DISGUISE ALWAYS THE BIGGEST **FREAK SHOW?**

BEYOND THE FACT THAT IT'S AGAINST THE LAW FOR HUMANS TO DO MAGIC, THE ROYALS MAKE IT AWFUL TOUGH FOR US. SO WE LIVE OUT HERE IN SECRET. THERE'S ABOUT TWENTY **HUMAN VILLAGES** IN THE FORESTS. WE STAY CONNECTED AND LOOK OUT FOR ONE ANOTHER.
THAT IS **WONDERFUL.**
IT'S **A LOT** OF HARD WORK, BUT WE'VE ALSO BEEN **VERY** FORTUNATE. WE PRETTY MUCH GO **UNNOTICED** BY THE MAGICAL PART OF THE WORLD.
YOU TRY THIS? IT'S **DELICIOUS.** IT TASTES LIKE **JOOK.**
JOOK?
IT'S LIKE A RICE PORRIDGE.
D.J.'S FAMILY MAKES IT ALL THE TIME.
THAT'S ONE OF YOUR **FRIENDS,** RIGHT? WE'RE GONNA GET SOME **SUPPLIES** TOGETHER FOR YOU ALL BEFORE YOU HEAD OUT TO FIND THEM.

THAT'S OKAY. YOU'VE DONE **MORE** THAN ENOUGH.
OH, WE **KNOW** YOU DON'T NEED MUCH HELP FROM US. MAGICAL HUMANS AND ALL, BUT WE CAN **AT LEAST** PACK YOU SOME SNACKS.
I WOULDN'T SAY **NO** TO A **BUCKET** OF THIS **JOOK!**
THEY ARE VERY **KIND.** AND **RESOURCEFUL.**
AND I'M FEELING **MUCH** BETTER. WE CAN START MAKING OU WAY TO THE C I THINK W

WHAT'S WRONG?
THEY SEEM **HAPPY.** AND I'M **SURE** THE OTHER VILLAGES ARE THE SAME. THEY'RE DOING **REALLY** WELL.
AND?
WE'RE GOING TO TRY TO TURN THE WORLD **BACK** TO THE WAY IT WAS BEFORE.

YES?
WHAT IF WE DO IT **WRONG?** WHAT IF WE MAKE IT **WORSE?**
BIRDIE.
NO. I **MEAN** IT. **LOOK** AT THEM. LOOK AT WHAT THEY'VE **MADE.**
THEY ARE **SAFE.** THEY ARE **HEALTHY.** THEY'VE MADE A **LIFE.**
THEY'RE MAKING **DO.** THEY'RE DOING THE BEST THEY **CAN** WITH WHAT THEY **HAVE.**

THEY LIVE IN A WORLD THAT'S AGAINST THEM.
WE'RE GOING TO GIVE THEM BACK THEIR WORLD. THESE ARE PEOPLE WHO HAVEN'T EVEN SEEN OR KNOWN WHAT THE WORLD COULD BE.
IT WAS TAKEN FROM THEM BEFORE IT COULD EVER HAPPEN.
WHAT IF WE MESS IT UP? WHAT IF WE FAIL?
YES. WHAT IF WE TURN IT ALL BACK, AND THE WORLD WINDS UP BEING WORSE? THAT'S THE RISK.
BUT YOU CAN'T SETTLE FOR A LESSER WORLD. YOU'VE GOT TO FIGHT FOR A BETTER ONE.
AND YOU CAN'T BE AFRAID OF FAILING.

NOT TRYING... IS WORSE.
WHEN I CAME THROUGH THAT PORTAL AND SAW THE CITY, AND I HAD THE OPPORTUNITY TO BECOME THE LOCK...
I KNEW I WAS GIVING UP MY LAST YEARS WITH OUR FAMILY. THAT WAS MY CHOICE.
IT WAS MY SACRIFICE. BECAUSE I KNEW I WAS THE ONLY ONE WHO COULD DO IT.
YOU. ME. AND YOUR FRIENDS HAVE A RESPONSIBILITY. WE KNOW THAT IF WE TRY REALLY HARD... WE CAN MAKE THINGS BETTER.
WE HAVE TO TRY.

TELL ME **REALLY...**
WHO ARE YOU?
HILO.
NOT **YOU.**
YOUR **GHOST.**

I'M NOT A GHOST.
SHE SAID SHE'S NOT A GHOST.
AND SHE SAYS WHO SHE IS ISN'T AS IMPORTANT AS WHO YOU REALLY ARE.
WHO I AM?
YES.
WHAT DOES THAT MEAN?
STOP IT.

WHAT DID SHE SAY?
SHE SAID WE **BOTH** NEED TO STOP **PRETENDING** AND FACE THE TRUTH.
WHAT'S THE **TRUTH?**
GET AWAY FROM HIM.

NOW.
WHO ARE YOU?
WE'RE ALL KINDS OF TROUBLE, SISTER!
HEY, Y'ALL! NICE DISGUISES! WELCOME TO THE DUNGEON!
ARE YOU OKAY?
YES. BUT DO YOU HAVE ANY FOOD? ALL THEY HAD WERE MACAROONS.
GROSS.
RIGHT?

ARE YOU THE **CLEANING CREW?**
MORE LIKE THE ONES WHO'LL BE MESSING THINGS UP IF YA TRY ANYTHING **FUNNY!**
IT'S OKAY, PIP. SHE'S NOT GONNA HURT US.
PIP IS **CUTE.**
HUSH.
WHO ARE YOU TALKING TO?
YOU.
HILO.

I'M TALKING TO **IZZY.**
YOU'RE **TALKING** TO HER BECAUSE YOU STILL **FEEL** LIKE SHE'S **WITH** YOU?
NO.
I'M TALKING TO HER BECAUSE... SHE'S **REALLY** HERE.

HERE?
WELL, NOT **HERE.**
HERE.

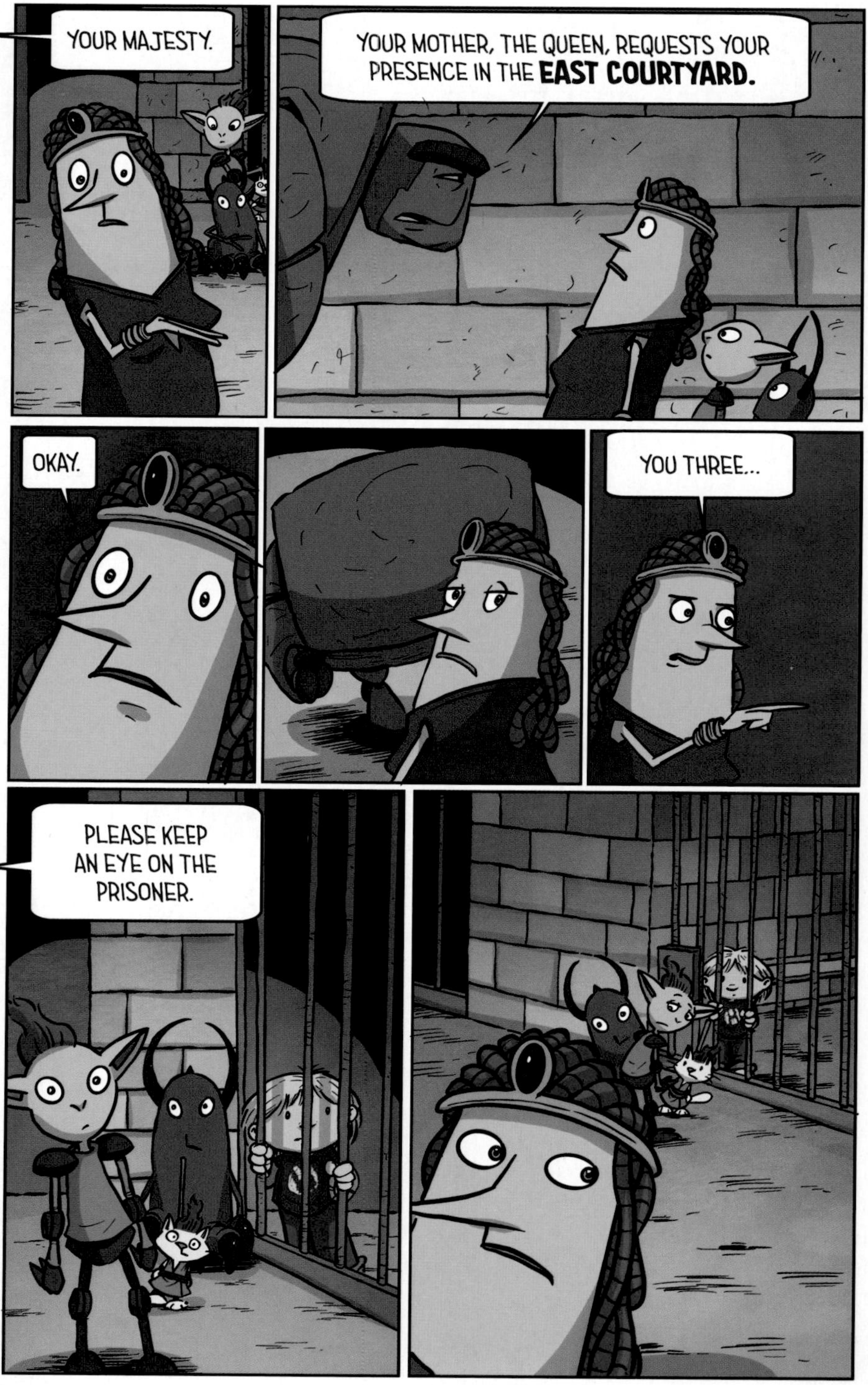
YOUR MAJESTY.
YOUR MOTHER, THE QUEEN, REQUESTS YOUR PRESENCE IN THE **EAST COURTYARD.**
OKAY.
YOU THREE...
PLEASE KEEP AN EYE ON THE PRISONER.

CHAPTER 9

THIS AIN'T NO PARTY

MOM! ARE YOU KIDDING ME?!
YOU WANT TO HAVE OUR CORONATION IN AN EMPTY COURTYARD?!
THIS IS NUTS, MOM! WE'RE SUPPOSED TO HAVE IT IN THE ROYAL STADIUM WITH A HUNDRED THOUSAND PEOPLE WATCHING!
AND WE'RE NOT READY TO SPELLCAST IT! HOW ARE PEOPLE GONNA WATCH IT AT HOME?! THAT'S SEVEN BILLION VIEWERS WHO AREN'T GONNA SEE ME BECOME KING!!
AND I'M STILL DECIDING ON APPETIZERS! HAVE YOU TRIED THESE MINI EGGROLLS?! THEY'RE TERRIBLE!!

THIS ISN'T A **PARTY.** THIS IS OUR **FATE.** THIS IS OUR **LIVES.**
WHAT ARE YOU **TALKING** ABOUT? IT **IS** A PARTY. YOU PUT **CROWNS** ON OUR HEADS. **WE'RE** THE NEW LEADERS, AND THE **WHOLE** PLANET CELEBRATES.
RIGHT?

YOUR MAJESTY, IF YOU BEGIN THE SPELL, **EVERY** BARRIER AROUND THE CASTLE WILL **DROP.**
YOU **ALL** WILL BE AT **GREAT RISK.**
RISKIER THAN **LOSING** THE WORLD?
THOSE MAGICAL HUMANS ARE **COMING** FOR US.
WE **HAVE** TO END THIS **NOW.**
KURACK
THE CORONATION IS... **A SPELL?**

WAIT--
IZZY IS IN YOUR **HEAD?**
NOT REALLY.
BUT YES.
BUT YES. SHE'S IN MY HEAD.
CAN WE GET HER **OUT?**

CAN WE MAKE HER A NEW **BODY?**
I CAN MAKE A SMALL **POSSUM** WE CAN PUT HER IN! IT COULD GET **MESSY!** IT **MIGHT** HAVE EXTRA LEGS.
I DON'T WANT TO BE A POSSUM. AND I **CAN'T** GET OUT.
SHE SAYS THAT WON'T WORK.
WHEN DID SHE WIND UP IN YOUR HEAD?
PROBABLY WHEN **WE** BROKE THE WORLD.
OH.
HEY.

HELLO.
WE'RE **BOK** AND **CHOI.** WE'RE THE NESTOR WHO ACCIDENTALLY GOT YOUR ENTIRE PLANET TAKEN OVER BY MAGIC.
WE REMEMBER YOU.
OI! NESTOR!
HELLO!
YES. WE'D LIKE TO HELP FIX EVERYTHING.

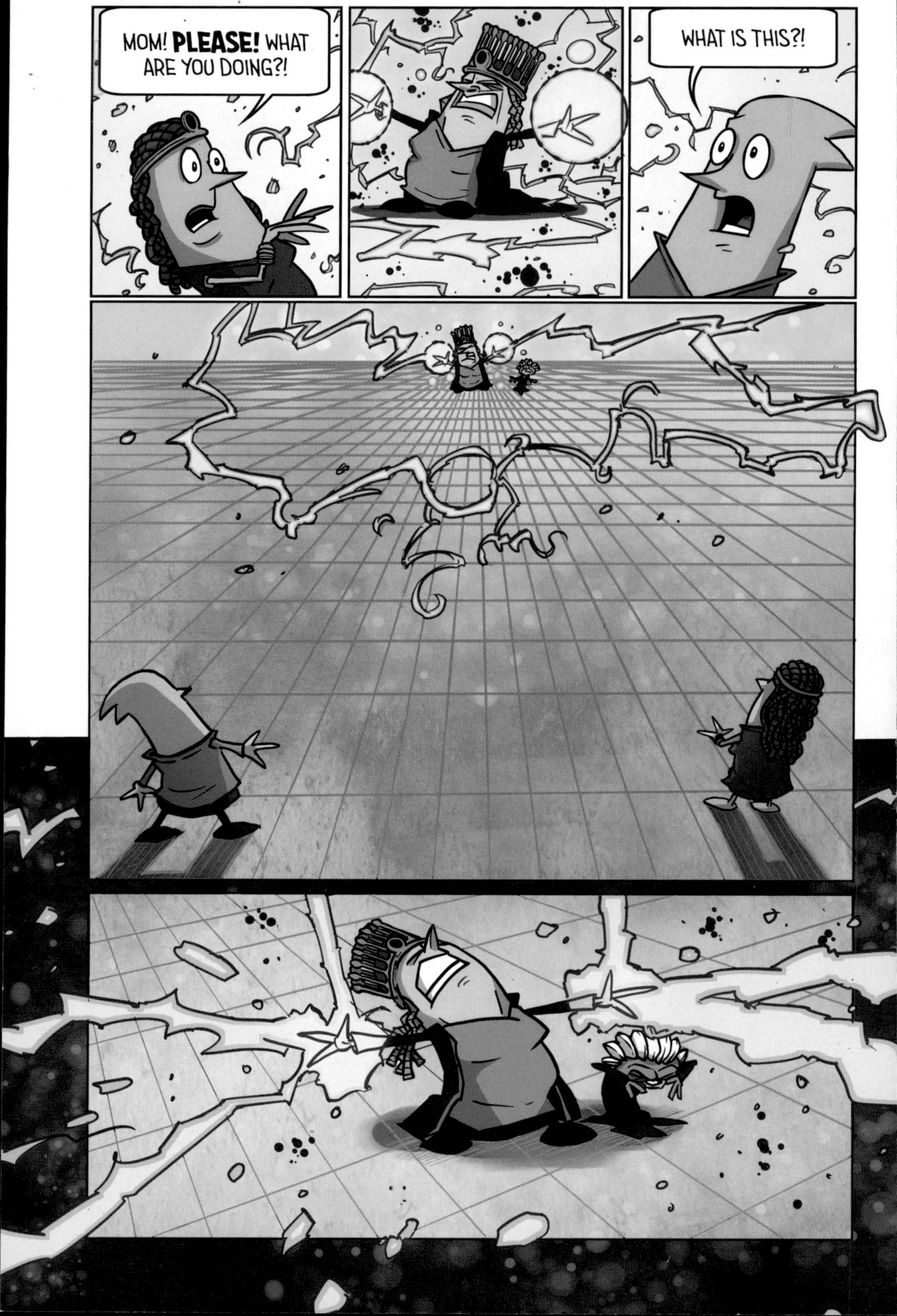
MOM! PLEASE! WHAT ARE YOU DOING?!
WHAT IS THIS?!

CREEEEEOOM

WHAT'S GOING ON?
I DON'T KNOW.
WHAT DOES IT **FEEL** LIKE TO **YOU?**
THERE'S SOMETHING HAPPENING AT THE **CASTLE.**
THE BARRIER IS **GONE.** I CAN TELEPORT YOU TO THE CASTLE NOW.
WHAT?

"YOU REMEMBER WHEN WE FELL THROUGH THE PORTAL. WELL, WE **THOUGHT** IT WAS GOING TO TAKE US BACK IN **TIME.**"
"BUT WE LANDED IN **THE MAYHEM.**"
THE CITY?
SOME CALL IT THAT, YES.

WE REALIZED THAT EARTH WAS PROTECTED BY A LOCK AND TIME TRAVEL WOULDN'T WORK. IT WOULD ONLY DELIVER US RIGHT TO THE CITY.
YES. THE POWER OF THE LOCK IS SERIOUS MAGIC.
SO WE WERE JUST GOING TO COME BACK TO YOU ALL, THEN...
IT FELT LIKE THE CITY... GRABBED US.

OUR NATURE, OUR POWER IS THAT IT HELPS ANYTHING MAGICAL GET STRONGER.
YES. WE ARE MAGICAL BOOSTER ROCKETS.
AND WHEN SOMEONE IS USING US TO BOOST THEIR POWER, IT FEELS LIKE WE'RE GETTING GRABBED.
THE CITY GRABBED US.
SLOW DOWN. THE CITY CAN'T BE USING YOU TO BOOST ITS POWER. IT'S A PLACE. IT'S NOT ALIVE.
IS IT?

I DO NOT KNOW. BUT IT GRABBED US. AND THEN--
THE CITY GRABBED SOMETHING ELSE.
"AND THEN... THE WORLD CHANGED."
RDWAB
WHAT ELSE DID IT GRAB? I--
D.J.?! LISA?!

MR. AND MRS. COOPER?
GINA'S FAMILY.
ARE YOU ALL RIGHT?
JUST LOCKED UP IN A **DUNGEON.**
CAN YOU HELP US WITH THAT?

BOOM
YES. WE CAN HELP WITH THAT.
JAILBREAK, BABY!
NOW, WHO WANTS TO GO FIGHT SOME MONSTERS?!
I DO.
ME TOO.
WAIT, THEY DON'T MEAN ACTUALLY FIGHTING MONSTERS, RIGHT?

CHAPTER 10

STOP HORSE

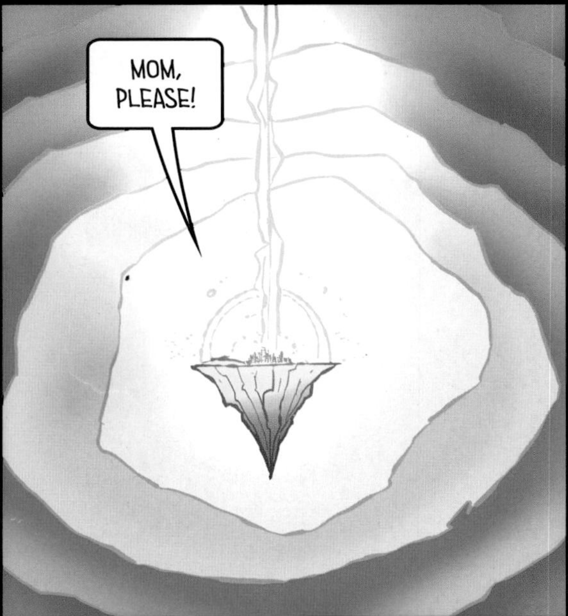

JUST TELL US WHAT THIS IS ABOUT!
WE CAN HELP YOU IF YOU TELL US WHAT YOU'RE DOING!
EVERYTHING WILL MAKE SENSE SOON! I PROMISE!
I'M DOING THIS FOR US!

POINK
BOOMF
STOP HORSE.
HELP US! **PLEASE!**

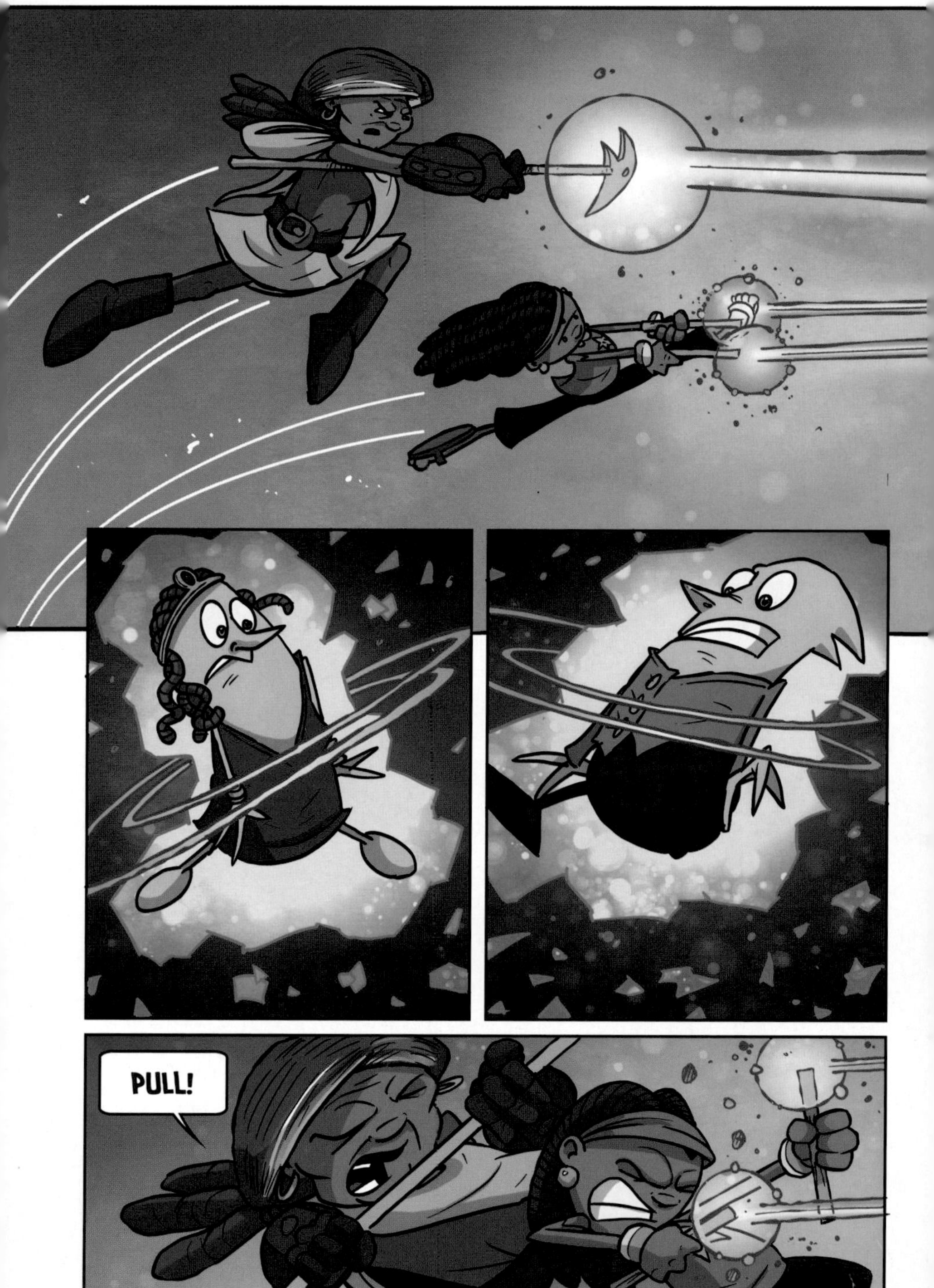
PULL!

NO!
NO!

NOOOOOO
HWEEEEEEEEE

POLLY?
GINA?
GINA!!
POLLY!

YEAH! IT'S US! AND **YOU** HAVE **A LOT** OF **EXTRA** PEOPLE WITH YOU!

PLEASE! WE NEED TO LEAVE HERE!
WE'RE NOT GOING **ANYWHERE** WITH THIS HUMAN GARBAGE!
ASH! ZACH! **STOP THIS!**

SALLY!

BOOMF
NO!
WHERE DID THEY GO?
YOU **KNOW** WHERE THEY WENT.

THE CITY.
WHERE ARE WE?
THIS IS WHERE ALL MAGIC USED TO TRY AND GET THROUGH BEFORE COMING TO EARTH.
I CALLED IT THE CITY. AND IT'S VANISHED.
GRANDMA REGGIE?
OH. YEAH. SORRY, DAD. THIS IS GREAT-GREAT-GREAT-GRANDMA REGGIE.

SHE'S AN INCREDIBLY POWERFUL SORCERESS WHO'S BEEN PROTECTING THE EARTH FROM MAGIC FOR HUNDREDS OF YEARS.
DARLIN'. I KNOW IT'S A LOT TO TAKE IN, BUT YOU'RE JUST GONNA HAVE TO CATCH UP.
OKAY.
THAT'S MY GREAT-GREAT-GRANDMA REGGIE.
I HEARD.
SHE'S, LIKE, A HUNDRED AND TWENTY YEARS OLD.
YES, DAD.

AND SHE'S BEEN **PROTECTING** THE **EARTH.**
WE HEARD.
I'M KIND OF FREAKING OUT.
WE KNOW.
SHE'S **QUITE** IMPRESSIVE.
YES. WE WEREN'T INTRODUCED. WE ARE **THE NESTOR.** WE BROKE THE WORLD.
HELLO.
HI.
STILL FREAKING OUT.
YES. DO YOU HAVE ANY SNACKS?

SOMETHING FEELS **WEIRD.**
I KNOW THIS PLACE.
I KNOW IT... **SO** WELL. LIKE...
I'VE BEEN HERE BEFORE.
YOU **HAVE.**
SHE SAYS THAT YOU HAVE.
WHO SAYS?
IZZY.

IZZY?!
IZZY'S IN HILO'S HEAD.
YOU FEEL LIKE SHE'S IN YOUR HEAD?
IZZY?
YEP. HILO'S SISTER.
HE SAYS THAT IZZY'S REALLY HERE.
WHERE?
IN HIS HEAD.

YOU'RE ACTUALLY **TALKING** TO HER? LIKE, SHE'S ALIVE--IN YOUR **HEAD**--YOU'RE NOT JUST SEEING **MEMORIES** OR SOMETHING?
NO. SHE'S HERE.
I'VE NEVER BEEN HERE!
I DON'T EVEN KNOW WHAT THIS PLACE **IS!** WHY DOES IT **FEEL** LIKE...
IT FEELS LIKE YOU **BELONG** HERE.

CROOM
ASHLINASCENT! YOU'RE COMING WITH ME RIGHT NOW.
NO, MOTHER! I WANT THE TRUTH!
WHY DO I KNOW THIS PLACE?! I'VE NEVER BEEN HERE!
HAVE I?!

NO ONE IS GOING ANYWHERE UNTIL WE GET ANSWERS.
YES! TELL ME, MOTHER! TELL ME RIGHT NOW!
UH-OH.
YES. SOMEONE IS GRABBING US.

TELL ME NOW!
WELL. THAT'S TERRIFYING.
YOUNG LADY! YOU WILL NEED TO CALM DOWN!
BREEN

SHE'S GOING TO **HURT** THEM! I **KNOW** SHE DOESN'T WANT TO DO THAT!
CAN'T **YOU** STOP HER FROM USING **YOUR** POWER?!
NO. WE WOULD NEED TO GET **FAR** AWAY FROM HER TO DO THAT.
IF SHE REMEMBERS WHO SHE **REALLY** IS, IT WILL SET **EVERYTHING** RIGHT.
BUT **YOU** HAVE TO REMEMBER TOO.

WHAT IS IZZY **SAYING** TO YOU?
A LOT OF STUFF THAT I DON'T UNDERSTAND.
I WANT TO TALK TO IZZY.
HOW?
YOU CAN DO SOMETHING, RIGHT?
NO.
BUT THE **THREE** OF US CAN.

TWEEEEEEEEEEEE

WHERE ARE WE?
IS THE SUN A MANGO?
THERE'S MANGOES EVERYWHERE.
OH.
WE'RE IN YOUR HEAD.
REALLY?

REALLY.
OUTSTANDING.
AND, YOU KNOW, KIND OF CREEPY.
LOOK!
CLICK

CREEEK
HEY!
DO YOU WANT TO COME IN?
I'VE GOT **MANGO SMOOTHIES!**

CHAPTER 11

THE LAST CITY ON EARTH

IT'S SO **NEAT** TO HAVE YOU HERE.

WHUMP

MANGO SMOOTHIE?
YES PLEASE.
IZZY. SO THIS IS YOU?
YES.
IZZY... YOU DIED.
YES.
SO YOU'RE A GHOST?

SHE'S NOT A GHOST.
BUT I AM KIND OF A GHOST.
YOU'VE BEEN SAYING THAT YOU'RE NOT A GHOST.
WELL, THIS IS ME WITHOUT A BODY. JUST MY THOUGHTS. MY FEELINGS.
I'M LIKE A HARD DRIVE WITHOUT A COMPUTER.
I'M THE AIR THAT'S INSIDE A BALLOON. BUT NO BALLOON.
I'M EVERYTHING THAT MAKES ME ME. EXCEPT I'M STUCK INSIDE YOU.

THEN **WE** NEED TO GET YOU **OUT.**
NO. I CAN'T GET OUT. I CAN **ONLY** EXIST IN **HERE.** I KIND OF **GREW** BACK.
GREW BACK?
YES. THERE WAS A **HUGE** PILE OF **ENERGY,** AND I GREW **AROUND** IT SO IT WOULDN'T GET LOST.
BUT **MOST** OF THE ENERGY GOT **TAKEN.**
AND **THAT'S** HOW THE WORLD GOT **BROKEN.**

I DON'T UNDERSTAND.
I THINK **I** DO.
GINA, **YOU** NEVER BROKE THE WORLD.
I THINK **I** DID.
NO YOU DIDN'T.
BUT YOU KINDA DID.

ASH, **PLEASE!** I WAS DOING THIS **ALL** FOR **YOU!** FOR **US!**
LIAR!
WELL, FROM WHAT I SAW, YER MUM WAS DOING A **SPELL** THAT INVOLVED ALL **THREE** OF YOU.
YES. **ALL THREE.**
MOTHER! WHAT WAS THAT **SPELL?!**

HOW DID HILO BREAK THE WORLD AND LET MAGIC TAKE OVER?
HE LEFT ALL THE ENERGY JUST LYING AROUND. THE SAME ENERGY THAT BROUGHT ME BACK LIKE THIS.
IZZY, WHAT ENERGY?
THAT ENERGY.
THAT'S... THAT'S THE EMPATIS.
THE POWER THAT MADE YOU AND ME.

YEP. SOME OF IT.
THERE USED TO BE A LOT MORE, BUT THEY TOOK IT.
WHO TOOK IT?
STOP LYING! TELL ME WHAT YOU DID!
IT'S NOT A LIE! IT'S OUR TRUTH!
I MADE A MACHINE THAT TOOK MY EMPATIS ENERGY AND GAVE IT TO YOU. IT MADE YOU INTO A HUMAN BEING.

BUT THERE WAS MORE. YOU WEREN'T SUPPOSED TO JUST BE A HUMAN BEING.
THERE WAS SO MUCH MORE POWER THERE. POWER THAT WAS MEANT FOR YOU TO USE!
YOU COULD'VE TOLD ME.
I THOUGHT YOU KNEW.
SO, WAIT-- THE POWER OF THE EMPATIS--THAT HUGE POWER SOURCE THAT MADE YOU BOTH INTO ROBOT SUPERHEROES-- WAS JUST...
...FLOATING OUT IN THE ATMOSPHERE.
UNTIL SOMEBODY TOOK IT.

CRUD AND SCRAMBLED EGGS.
WHERE ARE YOU GOING?!
BACK OUTSIDE! OUT OF HILO'S HEAD!
"I KNOW WHAT HAPPENED."
MOTHER, WHAT WAS THAT SPELL?!
I WAS PROTECTING US!

WHAT ARE YOU PROTECTING US FROM?!
THE TRUTH!!
HOOOON
THE TRUTH ABOUT WHAT?
THE TRUTH ABOUT... **WHO WE ARE.**

OH NO.
IT'S **YOU.**
WHO?
THE ROYAL FAMILY.
WELL... THEY HAVEN'T ALWAYS BEEN... **PEOPLE.**
THEY WERE A **PLACE.**
THIS PLACE.

YOUR **FAMILY** IS REALLY **THE CITY.**
THE CITY **ISN'T** GONE.
IT'S RIGHT HERE.
IT'S **YOU.**

MOM...
IS THAT TRUE?
IT WAS AN ACCIDENT.
YOU SEE, **THE NESTOR** FELL INTO THE CITY, AND IT WAS THE **FIRST** TIME ANY NESTOR **EVER** CAME THROUGH THERE.

AND IT **BOOSTED** THE MAGICAL POWER OF THE ENTIRE LAND.
WE SUDDENLY FELT **ALL** THIS **POWER,** AND WE KNEW...
WE COULD BE MORE THAN JUST A **PLACE.** WE COULD **REALLY** BE **ALIVE.**
SO, WITH A LITTLE BOOST, WE **REACHED OUT...**
IT REACHED OUT WITH THE **NESTOR'S POWER...**
... AND TOOK THE ENERGY OF THE **EMPATIS.**

AND WE WERE ALIVE.
THE EMPATIS MADE US INTO A FAMILY. A LIVING FAMILY.
AND WE WERE STRONG.
THEY REMADE THE WORLD.

A WORLD WE COULD LIVE IN. WHERE WE COULD BREATHE THE AIR. WALK WITH THE GRASS BENEATH OUR FEET AND STARE UP AT THE SKY.
A WORLD WHERE WE COULD DO MAGIC, NOT JUST BE PART OF IT.
YOUR FATHER AND I MADE THIS INTO A WORLD OF MAGIC. ERASED YOUR MEMORIES.
AND TOOK THIS WORLD.
I GUESS... I ALWAYS KNEW THIS A LITTLE BIT. MAYBE THAT'S WHY I'VE ALWAYS BEEN A LITTLE BIT ANGRY.
MAYBE I KNEW THAT THIS WAS A LIE.

SO... WE'RE NOT **REAL?**
OF COURSE YOU'RE **REAL.**
YOU HAVE **SERVED** THIS WORLD. **PROTECTED** THIS WORLD.
AND YOU ARE **EXTRAORDINARY.** AND **BEAUTIFUL.** AND **POWERFUL.** AND VERY MUCH ALIVE. YOU ALWAYS HAVE BEEN.
BUT NOT ALIVE LIKE **THIS!** NOT WHERE WE COULD LAUGH, AND RUN, AND BE **TOGETHER!**

THIS LIFE... IT WAS SO **LOVELY.**
"BUT IT BECAME **HARDER** TO STAY IN THESE FORMS. WE ALMOST TURNED **BACK** INTO THE CITY."
YOUR **FATHER**... HE GAVE UP ALL HIS ENERGY TO US SO **WE** COULD GO ON.
HE'S **STILL** HERE WITH US.
AND THE CORONATION SPELL?
IT WAS GOING TO MAKE EVERYTHING **PERMANENT.** WE WERE GOING TO BE ABLE TO STAY LIKE THIS **FOREVER.**

BUT, MOM, THIS **ISN'T** WHO WE ARE.
NO.
YOU ARE **SO** IMPORTANT TO THE WORLD. EARTH CAN'T BE WHAT IT'S MEANT TO BE WITHOUT **YOU.**
YOU NEED TO BE WHO YOU **REALLY** ARE.
YOU NEED TO BE WHO YOU **REALLY** ARE.
YOU **NEED** TO TAKE YOUR POWER BACK.

BUT THEN YOU'LL DISAPPEAR.
I'LL **ALWAYS** BE HERE.
BUT THEN WE'LL DISAPPEAR.
NO. YOU'LL **ALWAYS** BE RIGHT HERE.
BUT YOU NEED TO DO THIS SO THE WORLD CAN COME BACK.

NO.
SOMEONE'S **GRABBING** US AGAIN.
BOOM

KA-COOM
I **THINK** THERE'S PROBLEMS OUTSIDE!!

HWOOSH

EVERYONE, HOLD ON TO SOMETHING!!
WHAT IS SHE DOING?!

SHE TORE OPEN A **DIMENSIONAL HOLE!**
SHE'S TRYING TO **ESCAPE!**
IF WE CAN'T LIVE **HERE** THEN THERE ARE **MILLIONS** OF **OTHER** UNIVERSES WHERE WE **CAN!**
MOTHER! **PLEASE!**
IF THEY LEAVE EARTH, IT'LL BE **CATASTROPHIC!** THE WORLD **NEEDS** THE CITY! EARTH WILL BE DESTROYED BY EVIL MAGIC WITHIN **A DAY!**

THEY HAVE TO STAY!
THEY HAVE TO BECOME THE CITY AGAIN!
WE'RE OUT OF TIME! YOU HAVE TO LET ME GO!
NO! WE'LL FIGURE SOMETHING OUT!
NO! WE WON'T!
HILO! I'LL ALWAYS BE WITH YOU! YOU KNOW THAT!
IT'S NOT THE SAME!

NO. BUT THERE'S **SO** MUCH YOU STILL HAVE TO DO. AND TO DO THAT, YOU HAVE TO BE **EVERYTHING** YOU'RE SUPPOSED TO BE.
AND YOU'LL **NEVER** BE ALONE!
NO! YOU WON'T. WE'RE **ALWAYS** GOING TO BE **TOGETHER.**
WE'RE **ALWAYS** GOING TO BE **TOGETHER!**
WE ARE A **FAMILY!** AND WE WILL LIVE **FOREVER!**

YOU CAN **STILL** BE TOGETHER! THE WAY YOU **ALWAYS** HAVE!
AND YOU CAN **PROTECT** THE WORLD! THAT'S WHO YOU **ARE!**
MOM. I CAN FEEL IT NOW. THIS WORLD **NEEDS** US.
NO!!
CLAP

REGGIE!!
HOLD ON! IT'LL BE OKAY!
THIS DOESN'T **LOOK** OKAY!!
IT WILL BE!
I PROMISE!
WE CAN'T LET THEM ESCAPE TO ANOTHER WORLD OR DIMENSION! WE HAVE TO **SEAL** THAT PORTAL!
HOW?!
THEN **CLOSE** IT!
IT HAS TO BE DONE FROM THE **OUTSIDE!** SOMEONE HAS TO GO **THROUGH** THE PORTAL--
I'LL HAVE TO DO IT!
BUT ONCE IT'S SHUT-- CAN YOU COME **BACK?!**
NO.

REGGIE-- NO!
YOU DON'T KNOW HOW TO DO THIS.
AND--
YOU'LL HAVE WORK TO DO HERE ON EARTH.
DO YOU UNDERSTAND WHAT I'M TELLING YOU?
YES.

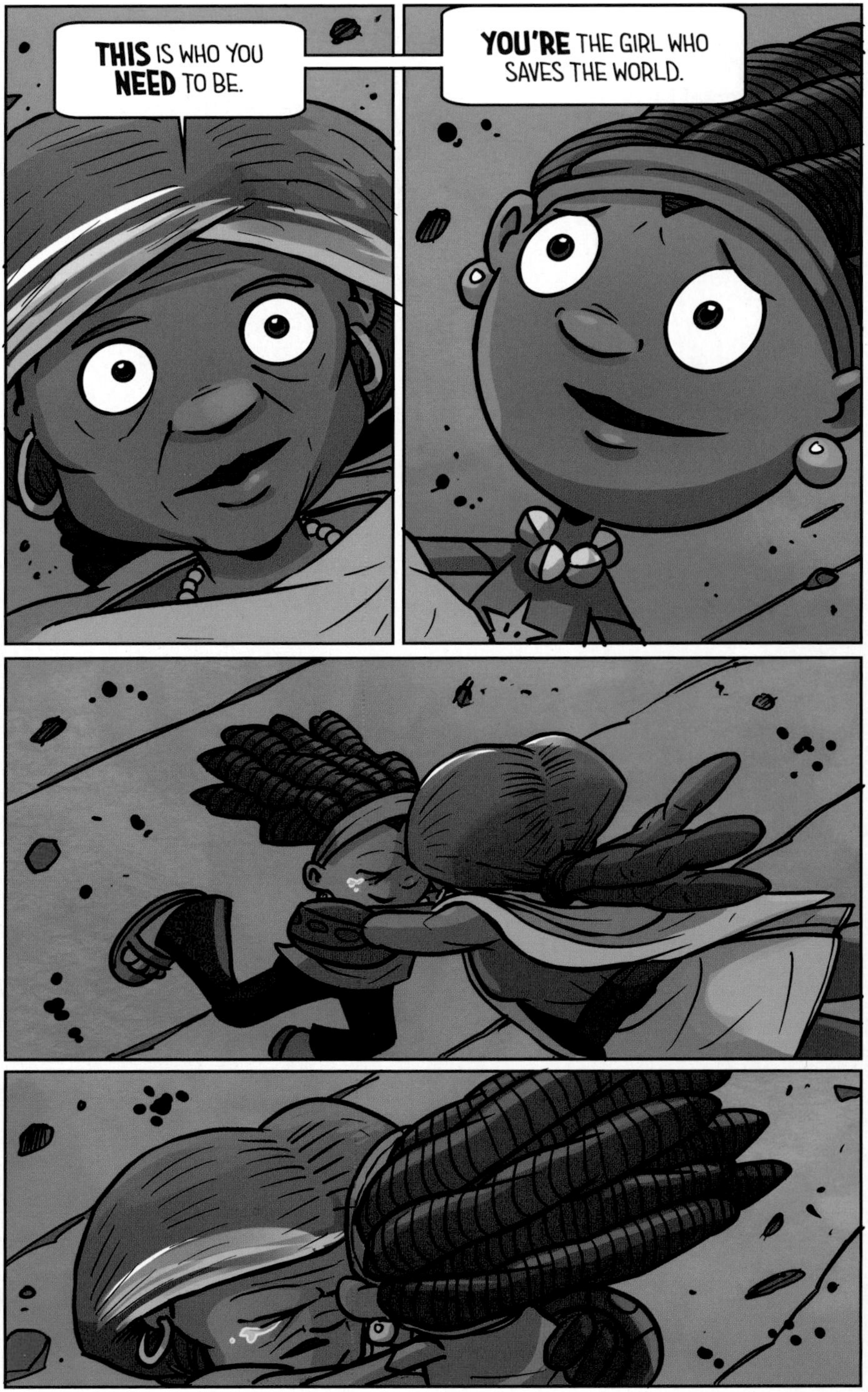
THIS IS WHO YOU NEED TO BE.
YOU'RE THE GIRL WHO SAVES THE WORLD.

IT'S TIME.
IZZY, I'M **SORRY!** I SHOULD HAVE BEEN ABLE TO SAVE YOU!

IT'S OKAY. YOU'RE GOING TO DO **SO** MUCH MORE.
YOU KNOW WHY?
BECAUSE YOU'RE **OUTSTANDING.**

NO.
IT'S OKAY, MOM. WE'LL DO IT TOGETHER.
AND WE WILL SAVE EVERYONE ON THE PLANET OVER AND OVER AND OVER AGAIN.
THAT'S WHO WE ARE.
I LOVE YOU.
WE LOVE YOU TOO.

YOU DID IT.
WE DID IT.
WE ABSOLUTELY DID IT!!
LOOK AT THIS.
IT'S BEAUTIFUL.
IT IS.
THANK YOU.
WHAT ARE YOU LOOKING AT?
HEY! WHERE'S HILO?
THAT'S WHAT I'M LOOKING AT.

IT SEEMS THAT I CAN FLY AGAIN.

TZOT
AND DO OTHER STUFF.
ARE YOU A ROBOT AGAIN?
NOPE. I'M HUMAN. I CAN JUST DO THINGS.
SUPERHUMAN THINGS.
YEAH.
THANK YOU, IZZY.

AND HEY! I TOOK A QUICK LOOK. THE WHOLE WORLD IS BACK TO NORMAL.
AND NO ONE WILL KNOW OR REMEMBER THAT ANY OF THIS HAPPENED.
EXCEPT US.
YES. EXCEPT ALL OF US.
WHERE'S REGGIE?
SHE... SHE CLOSED THE PORTAL.
SHE SAVED THE WORLD.
BUT SHE'S NOT COMING BACK.

WAIT. IF SHE'S GONE, WHO'S GONNA BE THE LOCK?
I AM.
NO.
D.J.
OH MY GOODNESS! WHAT AN HONOR!
YOU'RE GOING TO BE IN CHARGE OF PROTECTING THE WORLD FROM MAGIC?

NO. THAT'S NOT FAIR! WHY DOES IT HAVE TO BE YOU?!
I'M THE ONLY ONE.
WHAT'S WRONG? WHY ARE YOU-- WHY ARE YOU UPSET?
SHE CAN'T LEAVE.
SHE'S THE LOCK. SHE HAS TO STAY HERE.

NO. THAT... NO.
WE CAN VISIT, CAN'T WE?
NO. YOU CAN'T COME BACK. I DOUBT YOU COULD EVEN FIND YOUR WAY BACK HERE. AND YOU CAN'T STAY.
THE CITY AND THE LOCK MUST BE KEPT HIDDEN FROM THE WORLD.
NO. WE ARE GOING TO FIGURE THIS OUT.
I AM NOT LEAVING YOU HERE.

YOU DON'T HAVE A CHOICE.
IT WILL BE OKAY.

GINA!

GINA!!

OH.
HEY, EVERYONE.
MOM.
WHAT? WHAT'S **WRONG?**

MOM. IT'S GOOD TO SEE YOU.
IT'S GOOD TO SEE YOU TOO.
WHERE'S GINA?

HOOM
HWEEN
HWEEN

CHAPTER 12

SOMETIME LATER

LATER.
LATER.
LATER STILL...

LATER.
LATER.
LATER STILL...

REGINA COOPER.
HEY.

IT IS TIME FOR YOU TO LEAVE HERE.
SOMEONE ELSE IS GOING TO HAVE A TURN.
REALLY?
YES. YOU HAVE DONE SO MUCH AND PROTECTED THE EARTH SO WELL FOR A LONG TIME.
YEAH? TIME IN THE CITY IS KIND OF WILLY-DILLY.
I CAN'T TELL IF IT'S BEEN A MONTH OR YEARS OR A LIFETIME.
HOW LONG HAVE I BEEN HERE?

END OF BOOK NINE.

JUDD WINICK is the creator of the award-winning, **New York Times** bestselling Hilo series. Judd grew up on Long Island with a healthy diet of doodling, **X-Men** comics, the newspaper strip **Bloom County,** and **Looney Tunes.** Today, he lives in San Francisco with his wife, Pam Ling; their two kids; their cats, Troy and Abed; and far too many action figures and vinyl toys for a normal adult. Judd created the Cartoon Network series **Juniper Lee;** has written superhero comics, including Batman, Green Lantern, and Green Arrow; and was a cast member of MTV's **The Real World: San Francisco.** Judd is also the author of the highly acclaimed graphic novel **Pedro and Me,** about his **Real World** roommate and friend, AIDS activist Pedro Zamora. Visit Judd and Hilo online at juddspillowfort.com or find him on Twitter at @JuddWinick.

SOMETIMES THE UNIVERSE